UNDER HIS REIGN

WILLOW WINTERS

UNDER HIS REIGN

PROLOGUE

ALEC

At the Estate of the Authority

A SMALL KNOCK ON THE DOOR MAKES MY PEN slip on the paper. I tap it against my desk as I watch the door part and open. I knew she wouldn't wait for me to answer. My love, my beautiful little love. She pushes the door open with her gorgeous backside as she steadies the tray in her hands. An asymmetrical grin pulls at my lips. "You've brought me tea again? It's nearly midnight." I click the home button on my phone to double check—1:34 a.m. I close my eyes tightly and sigh in irritation. Time has gotten away from me yet again.

"It's chamomile, Alec. You need to relax"—Isabella gently places the silver tray on the edge of the desk before slipping her petite frame between my legs—"and come to bed." Her wide brown eyes find mine, as she lifts herself up to sit her lush ass in the center of the desk. I settle my forehead on her chest and wrap my arms around the small of her back. She runs her small hands through my hair and whispers, "Why don't you come to bed with me tonight?"

I pull away from her warmth to look into her gorgeous eyes. "You know why."

"But they're going to find out regardless of what we do. You can't stop it, Alec."

"They'll take you from me if they know how much you mean to me." My blue eyes plead with her to understand. I kiss the dip in her neck, just below her throat. We've had this same conversation over and over. Sighing deeper, I sit back in the leather seat, readjusting. A frown mars my face. As a sorcerer, I am never to love or have companionship. It clouds the visions and intentions. Never in my life did I feel tempted...until her.

"They're going to take me, Alec." Her tone is mournful but absolute. With her hand slipping over mine, she adds, "You are not taking advantage of the time we have now." Even as she states the tragic truth, happiness is evident on her face. She doesn't fear her death, but I do. I can't allow it to happen. I will do everything to protect her. Even if that means denying what I desire most.

"I can't risk you." I take her small hand in mine and kiss the gentle pulse of her wrist. She maneuvers herself and settles in my lap, wrapping her arms around my neck and kissing my cheek. Suppressing a groan of want and temptation, I resist moving at all. Not to pull her in closer and certainly not to push her away.

"It's not up to you. The seers are never wrong." I refuse to look at her as she speaks, so I stare at the back wall. It can't be true. I won't allow it to be true. The antique clock seems to tick louder and louder as I watch the time pass. There must be something I can do to prevent the fate the seers gave her. There's always a way.

Loving her is a death sentence. One we both knew when temptation beckoned us.

She tilts my head with her small and dainty fingers on my chin so I'm forced to look into her eyes. "They'll come for you once the war starts, and they'll find me." Her gaze searches mine. "You can't stop it, just like you can't stop this war."

My response is harsher than I intend. "I won't let them find you. I won't."

"So you'll keep me locked away?" Her warm breath and sultry voice harden my cock instantly. Her fingertip plays along my lips before traveling down my chin and throat until it reaches the dip of my throat. She leans into my ear and whispers, "Will you keep me chained, Alec?" The image of her naked and bared to me is my undoing.

"Do you want me to chain you, Isabella?" My tone is smooth and teasing, although my heart beats faster with lust.

"I want you to let me love you while I can." She scoots off my lap and onto the floor, settling between my legs. I place my hands on my thighs, my fingertips dig in, holding me still while she runs her hand over the bulge in my dark gray pants. Her firm breasts are pressed together, barely covered as the thin cloth of her linen robe slips down. Isabella is relentless in her need; she pushes my thighs farther apart.

"Bella." There's a trace of a warning in my voice, but she rises on her knees and places a gentle kiss on my chest just as the word leaves my mouth. The love in her action makes her name sound like a prayer as it passes by my lips.

When my eyes slowly open, I find hers still on me. "Please love me." Her bright eyes are filled with a sadness that's never there. My heart sinks and I immediately push the chair back, the legs grating on the old wood floors of my office. I get on my knees, carrying her with me, then cradle her face in my hand.

"You know I love you. I love you more than anything this world has for me." My lips are just inches away from hers. She must know how much I love her; every chance I see her, I tell her of my devotion. She's my world, my everything. I search her eyes for the acceptance of my words, but tears brim there instead, and I feel a tightness in my chest; a hard lump grows in my throat.

"Then make me yours, Alec." Her head falls against my shoulder as sadness overwhelms her. I wrap my strong arms around her and kiss her hair as she buries her face into my chest. Her small body shakes in my arms. Pain flows through me. I've never questioned anything in my life. I've been granted so much power, so much wealth, and so much control. Every action has been made with determined intent. But she weakens my resolve, clouds my thoughts, and makes me question everything.

"Bella, once we start this…" She leans into me, her breasts heaving with her every breath.

"I know." Her wide eyes plead with me. "I know, Alec, and I still want it. I only want you."

I pull us both up and sit back in my chair with her on my lap. I take her lips with mine and bring her legs to straddle me, so I can rock myself against her. I'm rewarded with a gentle moan, the most pleasurable sound. Her fingers pull at my hair as her mouth devours mine. With a possessive grip on her hips, I rock her against me, teasing both of us. "Please," she whispers in the air between us, gasping for breath.

Hearing those words on her lips is what brings me to fold. She will be my undoing. I know this, yet I can't help myself.

With one arm under her ass, I carry her. I use the other arm to wipe everything off my desk. It scatters recklessly as my heart rages and adrenaline scorches my veins.

"I've wanted to take you on my desk every day you've stepped foot in my office." I pull away from her as I set her on the desk and slowly take my clothes off. Her heavy breathing and the blood rushing in my ears are all I can hear as I unbuckle my pants. She watches, her pouty lips dropping as my clothes fall to a puddle on the floor. She follows suit, slipping off her robe and revealing herself. I can't resist her. Her lush, pale breasts fit my hands perfectly. Her soft, pink nipples are small and peak easily as I pinch them between my fingers and pull, marveling at how perfectly they harden. She bites into her bottom lip, her head falling forward as I toy with her. I lean down and take one nipple in my mouth as she arches her back and moans.

As I lose suction, I pull back and let it pop out of my mouth.

"Alec," she moans and I tisk her, "Quiet." I rub her clit through the thin lace that's soaked with her arousal. "You'll be quiet, won't you, my little love?" The vampires are gone, no longer on the estate, but I can't allow anyone to hear.

This is for us. Only for us.

"I'll be quiet, Alec. I promise." She squirms, eager and wanton.

"Be still." Her lips part as I pull my hand away to gently remove her undergarment. "Lie back and spread your legs for me."

She easily obeys. Her blonde hair lays like a halo around her and her hands pinch her nipples, keeping them hard. The sight of her pleasuring herself has my dick harder than steel and begging to be inside of her. I lean down and suckle her clit while pushing a finger inside. Her hymen keeps me from fully entering her and makes me groan against her heat. Her tight walls pulse around my finger as she nearly reaches climax from just the vibrations of my groan on her clit.

"Good girl." I lick her arousal off my fingers as I pull back, towering over her, knowing all too well what I'm about to do. Planting soft kisses on her belly and up the curve of her waist, I finger fuck her, my thumb on her clit, until she comes undone for me. Her thighs shake and I nip her, not enough to leave a mark, but enough to stifle my groan.

A blush rises up her chest as I line up my dick. Her head thrashes with the waves of her orgasm overwhelming her. *I should do it now. I should rip through her virginity and take her while she's lost in pleasure.* The head of my dick stretches her walls as my thumb presses mercilessly against her clit. Her mouth parts and I know she's going to scream from the intense sensation, so I quickly cover her mouth with mine and thrust all of me into her. In one swift move, I take what's mine. Her back bows and I muffle her cries with my kiss. I'm still buried deep inside her and continue to rub her hardened nub. Her pussy pulses around my dick and slowly stretches to fit me.

I pull away slightly to look down at her. Her eyes are closed tightly as she continues to pant. Her skin is flushed a beautiful pink and her plump lips are parted. The sound of her shallow pants makes me worry that she's in too much pain. I nuzzle her neck and plant a small kiss on the crook of her neck. "More, my love?" I wait with bated breath. Her arms wrap around my back and her blunt nails dig into my shoulders, keeping me close to her. I fucking love it.

"Yes!" I pull back just enough for her to feel the loss and I fucking love how her pussy grips my dick, wanting to keep me inside of her. I pump in again, all while watching her expression of ecstasy. "More, Alec." She whimpers, keeping her eyes closed.

"Look at me." Her eyes open as I thrust in and out with a slow pace. I grab her calf and put it against my chest as I push deeper into her. I hit her cervix with each thrust, making her breasts bounce and small whimpers escape. *Fuck*, it feels so damn good. Her eyes stay on mine the entire time and I fucking love it. She bites her lip as I increase my pace. I pull her ass off the desk, just enough not to hinder my pace, and thrust in even deeper. She cries out and I lean down to catch the sound of her pleasure between my lips. I bite her bottom lip gently and continue rutting into her heat as I feel my balls draw up and my spine tingles with my impending release.

I pull back and watch her writhe under me. "You're such a good girl. Staring back at me like I told you to." My words set her off again and she struggles to obey as her body trembles beneath me. Her mouth opens as her pussy clamps down hard on me while she comes. A cold sweat breaks out along my skin as I find my own release. I push deep inside of her, filling her. My come leaks in between us and onto my thighs. I fucking love it.

I lean down to kiss her with every bit of passion I have as I struggle to catch my breath. She breaks our kiss to lean her head back and breathe. "I love you, Alec."

"I love you, Bella. I love you enough to do whatever it takes."

I'll never let them take her from me. Never.
I will burn the world before I let them take her.

CHAPTER 1

DRAGO

In the Castle of Silver Isle

THE SMACK OF OUR BOOTS AGAINST THE hard, black marble echoes as we make our way toward the throne room. The fire crackles in the torches perched on the smooth walls of the long hallway, and the sight of the orange embers and bright flames warms my chest. It's been too long since I've felt the need for fire.

"I don't know why you care what the sorcerer has to say," my brother mutters with disdain as we near the carved stone doors, shattering the small bliss I'd gained from the vision of the flames.

"I've grown bored, Cyrus." I roll my shoulders and crack my neck as my palms slam against the hard stone and part the doors for us. They swing open with a loud groan, granting us access to the massive room. Our thrones stand tall in the back of the room, bathed in the glowing light on the far wall. The intricate metal shines with wealth and power.

"Grown bored of luxury, Drago?" Although Galen's

tone is teasing, he knows just as well as I do that this castle is tiring. There's nothing of interest as of late and my inner beast craves a challenge.

"When was the last time you stretched your wings, Galen?" My brother narrows his eyes in irritation. "It's been far too long for me." Both brothers, one on either side of me, snort but fail to answer my question. I answer for them, "Nearly a decade."

"You're bored of luxury, yet I'm bored of fighting the weak." I resist the urge to roll my eyes at Cyrus's arrogance.

"Some fights were worthy." He huffs in amusement. "If they weren't, then there would be more than three dragons still in existence." It's a cold reminder and the chill of my words settles deep in my veins. The air around us grows thick as we separate and each take our place on our thrones. I take my seat in the center and enjoy the feeling of the hard, cold metal against my bare back. I strum my fingers along the arm of the throne and take in each of my brothers in turn.

Cyrus is the youngest by nearly a decade, although no one would know. The three of us are nearly identical in appearance even though we were birthed separate. My father's genes are strong; we're the spitting image of him. I remember his cold, dark eyes, nearly black, but they sparked red with his anger. We have his thick dark hair, sharp jawline, and high cheekbones. Our broad shoulders and hardened muscles complete the image of utter dominance and power.

"I see no point in any of this." Galen's cheek rests in his hand as he stares at the entrance to the dark room, waiting rather impatiently for our guest. The fire lit behind us adds a shadow to his face, making him appear even more angered and intimidating. The idea of his exasperation pulls a smirk to my lips.

"I agree." The hint of my smile falls at Cyrus's bland statement.

"You two used to be amusing." I allow my irritation to be apparent as I sit farther back in my seat and straighten my shoulders.

"I have no use for the sorcerer, nor the humans for that matter."

"It's not about possession, it's about the perception of power," I respond coldly to Galen's words.

His shoulders rise as Cyrus snorts a laugh. "Are you suggesting that our power is being questioned?"

"What power, Galen?"

His brows furrow and his pupils flatten, turning reptilian and sparking a pale blue. "What do you mean 'what power'?" He sneers his angered words, and they sound clear in the vast, cold room, echoing off the jagged stone walls. "No one dares to question our claim to this territory. We have more wealth than we have room to store it."

"Yes, but you miss my point, brother."

"And what is that, Drago?" Cyrus's curious voice utters his words carefully, as if testing out their taste before letting them pass his lips.

"We've been forgotten. You cannot perceive power

if you have no memory of it. We sit alone in our castle, enjoying the spoils of our wealth, but it's been too long brothers—far too long—since our names have been spoken."

"And this sorcerer?" Galen's disbelief is apparent. "What does he have to offer us?"

I wave my hand aimlessly in the air. The sorcerer spoke vaguely of glory and wealth, but it didn't appeal much to me. "You dragged me from my chambers merely because of your boredom." Galen runs a hand down his face. "You need a hobby."

Cyrus's wicked eyes find mine as a stealthy grin forms on his face. "Or better yet, someone to warm your bed."

"If they don't heat for me than I'm not interested." My tone is flat.

"Since when?" Cyrus scoffed. Being the youngest of us, he hasn't grown bored of the women who throw themselves at us. Although we're feared, we're still de-sired. They long for expensive baubles and offer their bodies in exchange. Cyrus set a bad precedent on that front.

I used to give in to temptation, but it's been years since I've indulged. I want more now. I long for dragon-lings. Carrying a dragon is nearly impossible for mortals or other shifters. My brothers and I are the last of our clan and our species is sure to die with us. I may only look thirty years old, but I'm nearly two hundred. I'm growing old, and it's long past due for me to settle with a mate. A sigh leaves me in longing, and I run the pad of my thumb along my stubbled jaw.

In the last few years I've accepted that it's not meant to be. In the presence of dragons, women capable of carrying our seed display strong signs of ovulation, the most obvious is her heated core and strong scent. I've searched the kingdom for years for a woman who would be able to carry my young but have never found a woman to heat for me. Nor have my brothers. Unlike Cyrus, I've no desire to bed a woman for sport, and unlike Galen, I'm not bitter that the women capable of carrying dragonlings to term have disappeared with the remainder of our clan.

Galen sits farther back in his seat, getting comfortable. "If only a woman would heat for me, I'd fill her every chance I was given." As Galen's soft words settle in the emptiness of the vast throne room, a timid knock echoes off the walls.

"Enter." I bellow, and in response the large door cracks and slowly opens. A petite woman in a simple linen dress enters with her head bowed. One of the many servants in our quarters. Our kingdom is littered with humans, only those born into servitude are permitted to stay in the castle. They're permitted to leave if they'd like, but none do. We ensure their wellbeing just as much as their fear in us. Our kingdom is prosperous, but those who stay to serve us are given wealth far beyond the possibilities awaiting the commoners.

The woman walks obediently, her eyes on the floor

and her hands clasped in her front, stopping a few feet from the thrones and waiting as expected.

"You may speak."

The small woman raises her head and meets my gaze. Respect outweighs the fear in her eyes as she speaks confidently. "Your guests are here, my Lords." Her sweet voice is so soft it barely registers.

"See them in."

She nods. "Yes, my Lord."

Before giving her the command to leave, Galen speaks. "Adelle is it?" I commend him on his memory. We're introduced to the servants as they come and go through the castle, but it's been decades since I've learned a new name. Most I held dear have passed, and since then I find it difficult to form any bond with the humans. Although, judging from the young woman's age, I may see my death along with hers. For the second time today, I'm reminded of my age and oncoming mortality.

"Yes, my Lord." She remains calm and patient waiting for her orders.

"Speak more clearly next time." The young woman pales with fear at Galen's admonishment. Her bottom lip wobbles slightly, and I repress the need to roll my eyes. We wouldn't banish her for something so irrelevant, but we also don't squash the rumors that we would. "Understood?" His tone is hard and unforgiving although I'm sure he doesn't realize it.

Her breath hitches as she tries to get the word out. Watching her struggle to contain her mortification makes my stomach churn. I grant her a small mercy and send her back to her duties. "Our guests Adelle."

The little human nods instead of speaking and quickly turns to leave us. I turn my head to give Galen a death stare. "What?" he says with exasperation. "I could barely hear her." He rolls his eyes and throws his hands up. "Seriously, what must I do?"

Cyrus chuckles, deep and low as several steps are heard nearing us. Of the three of us, Cyrus is far better with human interactions. The three of us straighten in our seats and stare ahead as the doors part once again.

Adelle enters first, her eyes focused on the black swirled marble floor. The click of her tiny shoes is accompanied by the sounds of heavy boots from the three men trailing her. The first of the three I recognize as the sorcerer who sent word of his request, Victor Wade. His blond hair hangs past his shoulders, his sharp blue eyes stare straight, and a thin smile grows on his face. Few have seen the three of us in person with the exception of our servants and the women we keep. His eyes widen and spark with curiosity, but if he's under the impression that he'll be gaining information from this meeting, he's mistaken. I've granted him access solely to hear his offer. Purely out of boredom.

The other two men appear to be mere humans, although they may be weak sorcerers; I suppose they're assistants of his. Neither has qualities that allow them to stand apart from the norm. Adelle stands tall and proud at the side of the room. She stares straight ahead, showing no emotion and simply waiting for her instructions. She's been trained well and has recovered nicely from Galen's criticism. She's a worthy servant.

"My Lords." Victor bows slightly as do the other men. It's always humorous to me to see visitors bow. The more trouble they think they're in, the deeper they bow.

"Victor." I breathe deeply and wait for him to speak. For years, I've felt as though my wings have been clipped. It's time I got out of this rut and started living before my death is suddenly upon me. However, neither of my brothers seem truly interested in this conquest, and although I'm bored, I have no intention of going to war on my own. Cyrus may be interested, but more out of curiosity than a desire to fight.

"What is it you've come to offer us?" Cyrus's inquisitiveness has always gotten the better of him. It's my hope that with him on my side, Galen will be swayed.

Victor takes a nervous swallow before speaking with false confidence. "The Authority is a threat to all things supernatural." Before he can continue, he's rudely interrupted by Galen.

"I assume you have proof, and this is not a statement you'll leave with no support." Victor's obviously caught off guard, but he swallows his pride and continues.

"Have you not heard of the blood they were dealing to the vampires?"

"There's been talk of treachery." Or so we've heard. I hadn't given the whispers much consideration until I'd been given word of Victor's plan. "But from what I recall, the Authority is the one who put an end to that debauchery."

"Lies. It's all lies. I had allies within the Authority that have since been blamed and massacred."

"I was under the impression that Alec was your ally." My statement comes out as though it's a question. I already know the answer though. I'm more than prepared for this meeting, as I always am. Although we're across the world in our secluded territory, information is fed to us frequently on anything and everything that should catch our interest. We pay a healthy sum of gold for information that keeps us well informed. The whispers from our contacts in the Authority are what originally caught my amusement.

"He was. He is no longer." My eyes narrow as I take in his appearance. Beads of sweat line his brow, and he reeks of deceit and betrayal. I run my thumb over the tips of my fingers, considering how I'd like to play this. After all, if I send him away, I have nothing but vaults of hoarded treasure collecting dust to return to. They don't inspire life within me. They don't give me the same spark they once did.

Cyrus speaks before I'm able. "So you believe the Authority must be dismantled, and you would lead in its place?" From what I gather, Cyrus's assumption is correct. The words "rebellion", "war", and "dictatorship" resonate within me and wake my sleeping dragon. A low flame burns in my chest.

"I only ask for your aid if it will be needed." I scoff at his deceitful response.

"Do you think we wouldn't be needed?" I sit forward in the throne and stare into his fearful eyes. Bloodshed will occur no matter our involvement, but if we were to fight on their side, victory is certain.

"My Lord"—he lowers his gaze to the floor like a coward—"I do believe your assistance would be required." I lean back and sneer. It takes a moment before the sniveling fool raises his head to meet my gaze once again. Of course we would be required. There's no other reason he'd risk his life to see us. He *needs* us.

"There was some mention of gold, silver, and opal mines." Cyrus gets to the point although his tone holds little interest. Destroying other beings, no matter what their nature, is simple enough. What matters is what we'd receive in return.

"Yes." Victor nods his head enthusiastically, not realizing how little we care for our treasures at this point. There's only so much wealth you can acquire before it merely fades into the background.

"Not interested." Galen's slowly spoken words leave an air of disappointment clouding the men before us. But before I can speak, the sorcerer's vigor returns.

"Lord Arrington, if I may, there is something waiting in Shadow Falls that I believe you truly desire." He takes a hesitant step forward, a brave thing for him to do. I wave my hand willing him to continue. "There is word of a woman, merely human, but she's from a strong line of breeders."

My body sways forward with awareness, but Galen fails to see where this conversation is headed. He speaks with disdain, "What of this woman?"

"There are whispers among the healers that she's capable of carrying your young, my Lords." The breath stills in my lungs as the words hang in the air. The fire crackles behind us and the heat seems to intensify. "She's untouched, but she is known to have the fertility to carry many sons and daughters for you."

"Who is this woman?"

"Isabella Faye. She is held within the walls of the Authority, yet she is not claimed by anyone." My fists clench. I have eyes in the Authority, yet they haven't sent word of this. How is it that this sorcerer has information that I do not?

"What use do they have for a human?" My brows furrow and my jaw ticks. I'm not sure what to believe from this liar's lips, but the possibility of his words being true is enough to rouse the interest of all of us.

"It's rumored that Alec is keeping her captive, unbeknownst to her. He knows the line will end with you three. He spoke of this frequently to me."

"And what did you reply when he spoke of our demise?" An asymmetric grin grows on Cyrus's face, but I haven't the energy to laugh at his taunting. The possibility of her existence is enough to gain my desire for this conquest, and I'm hopeful it's enough for Galen as well. I watch him as Victor stumbles through a response. Galen's fingers gather his beard as he seems to contemplate his decision. I interrupt whatever babble Victor is attempting to speak to question my brother.

"What do you think?"

He hesitates only a moment, his fingers tapping in rhythm on the metal arm rest. "I'm intrigued. I will take a few days to consider." I respect Galen's decision. He's always careful in his deliberations; it's why the three of us remain living, so I will not push him. It will be easy to gather more information on whether or not Victor speaks the truth. I push the hope blooming in my chest down—deep down. I will not be made a fool of by a man of such low morals. No matter how much I crave what he offers.

"I understand." Victor clasps his hands in front of him and bows. "Before I go, I'd like to present you with parting gifts, if I may."

I nod slightly, and at my approval, he motions for the men accompanying him to leave and attain whatever these gifts are. I imagine it's gold. Others tend to think that's what we prefer.

Cyrus leans forward as Galen strums his fingers along his lip, no doubt contemplating the possibility of this *Isabella* being a mate. I catch Galen's eyes and hold them, watching as they quickly flash reptilian and flicker icy blue in color. His dragon craves the woman. I snort and nod as my own dragon claws against my chest. There's no need to fight over her, she will choose which of us she'd like to mate. My shoulders stiffen at the thought. I look back at my brother and he seems to be thinking the same.

Cyrus laughs and claps his hands to gain our attention. He smirks at us. "Maybe we should wait and see if this woman even exists?" I relax my posture and lean back once again.

"For once our little brother has a point." Galen huffs a puff of cold air and settles against the hard throne.

"We shall see." I won't show any mercy if Victor has brought false hope to us. It'll be his death.

As Galen settles his dragon, mine pushes furiously against me, urging me to free him. The move is one of fury and rage. I instantly rise out of the throne, frightening the sorcerer who cowers and lowers his head. My dragon settles and my forehead pinches in confusion. My breathing is uneven, and I take a moment to regain my composure. I search the room for a threat, but there is none. Adelle's eyes widen, but she remains somewhat poised. It's been quite some time since I've felt the push from my beast. I grunt and retake my seat, not know ing what the hell got him riled up. My eyes dart to the door as I hear the men enter the room, each followed by a woman.

The woman on the left and closest to Cyrus is a young, petite blonde, far too skinny and pale to be well. She stares at the floor as she walks. Her hands are shackled, and her breathing comes in short pants. The clacking of the metal chains banging together echoes through the empty hall. The red-headed woman on the right is no doubt of similar age and health. They're both in desperate need of a good meal and reek of fear and uncertainty. My nostrils flare in anger.

As the men plant their feet, the two women go gently to their knees and bow before us. Shackled and trained to submit. Victor has brought us slaves as a gift. I clench my fist and consider ending his life. The only reason I hesitate is the possibility of this *Isabella*. I shift uncomfortably as I decide what I want to do. He swallows thickly, sensing my anger.

"We have a third, my Lord." My brows raise in surprise. He thinks I'm angry that there are only two. What a stumbling fool. My jaw ticks, and my dragon attempts to leap from my chest once again, furiously batting his wings. The urge to leave the room is overwhelming. To go to *something*. The movement of my dragon distracts me for a moment as the doors open and a woman in chains is pushed through, stumbling and falling hard on her knees.

My dragon relaxes and pushes slowly against me, focusing only on the woman. Her dirty blonde hair is a tangled mess. She's in the same condition as the others, but she's different somehow. "Come!" Victor's hard command to her makes my dragon's fire burn in my chest.

Her eyes find mine as she raises her head. She spits her words. "I'd rather die." My heart flames and my blood heats. Her hard eyes of defiance light a deep, buried need within me. I rise and walk to her slowly.

"Bow to him." I ignore the sorcerer, striding by him and stalk the length of the hall.

"Fuck you!" She bites out the words through clenched teeth and the movement of her jaw emphasizes the bones sticking out from her skin. She's so thin. Far too thin. The spell of a whip cast by the man who dragged her in sings in the air as it pierces across her neck and down her shoulder, ripping into her soft flesh.

I snarl in anger and allow my dragon to come forth. Scales impale my skin and flow down my back as my jaw stretches and the heat of fire scorches my throat. I grip the man's throat and squeeze, digging my sharp talons in as my teeth sharpen and lengthen. I don't let my dragon fully take over; I merely allow his strength to show.

Fire smolders deep in my belly as I hiss flames through my teeth and scorch the man. He screams a strangled cry in agony. I'm only vaguely aware of the hushed gasps, it all happens so quickly. His flesh burns with a nauseating stench I'd almost forgotten as he struggles in my grasp. I don't let up on the fire consuming him until he's still and burned to a crisp. The hall is silent as ashes of his remains scatter. My eyes flash reptilian and I know they must be red as my dragon grants my human body control and the scales, talons, and fangs retreat. The pain is pleasurable. My dragon protests, but I am far stronger than he is. With a hiss and a snort of fire, my human form recovers. The bones crack into place and my head slowly turns to the focus of my ire.

Victor and the other man drop quickly to their knees.

"You will go and gather your army." Galen's command from his throne surprises me. "Now." The man and sorcerer stumble to rise, then leave quickly and silently, whispering their thanks. They should be dead.

I watch them leave before turning my attention back to the woman.

"Does she really mean that much to you?" I hear Cyrus ask Galen, gathering my attention.

"I'll let him live until I see this Isabella." I nod knowingly as a fire burns within me. Victor's days are numbered, but he may be useful in attaining this mate he speaks of.

Ever so slowly, I reach down to the woman who's seething in pain from the slash on her skin, kneeled over and trembling. Blood drips down her shoulder and I move to wipe it, to offer her comfort. Her hard eyes find mine and she grimaces. "I'll kill myself before I let you hurt me. I'll starve myself to death if you keep me caged." She swallows thickly, pain and stubbornness equally reflected. "I won't be your slave." Her throat is dry and her words are strangled, but her fight is commendable.

I smile down on her, loving the spirit she has. "I have no intention of you being a slave." It takes a moment to steady my breath as the tense air crackles between us. "What name do you go by?"

She stares at me with wide, wild eyes and slight disbelief and presses her lips together. Unwilling to believe me. Defiantly disobeying me. The words behind me are a distraction. Cyrus and Galen tell Adelle to feed the other women and grant them housing in the castle. Deliberately and carefully, I reach down to push the woman's hair out of her face and that's when I smell it.

Her heat.

I struggle to remain composed as my blood rushes and my heart beats chaotically. There's no way my brothers would be able to scent her so far away. I look over her small, damaged body and frantically smell her again. I have to resist the urge to flip her over and bury my nose between her legs.

"I hate you all." Her words barely hit me as I stare into her heated gaze.

She's fertile, but she may lose her heat as she stays within my proximity. It's happened before. A woman seems to heat for us, but it's not ours to take. It dies quickly and never returns. But this is the strongest I've ever scented a woman. There's a possibility that she's capable of heating for me. That she's intended for me. *Or one of us.* The thought makes me tremble with rage.

Mine! My dragon hisses in my chest.

"Take her to my bedchambers." I nearly choke on the loud words that escape my lips without my consent.

A shocked tone resonates behind me. "You can't be serious, Drago." Galen glares at me with disbelief as another servant enters and attempts to pick up the woman. My potential mate. I hear a scuffle and turn to see the servant stumble, but she doesn't fall.

She may think she can fight me, but she cannot.

"I'll do it." I grit out with irritation to the servant as

I turn my back on my brothers. I know if they find out she's in heat, there will be hell to pay. I grip the small blonde woman forcefully and pin her to my chest as she struggles against me.

"Drago!" Cyrus calls after me as I carry her away from them.

The woman cries out in my arms, wriggling her body. I ignore her attempts as I hear my heart beat louder and louder. The look of disgust on Cyrus's face makes me aware that he misunderstands my intention. I look over my shoulder at my brothers who stare back with confusion and incredulity.

My dragon hisses. My eyes flash reptilian and flames burn in my chest. My dragon wants her now, but he'll have to wait. I won't touch her until she's ready to carry my dragonlings. Her fists pound against my chest even as I hold her with a single arm. She's weak and frail.

"What are you doing, Drago?" Galen's words carry through the room, and I turn at the doors with the woman screaming in my arms.

"I'll come back and we will prepare for war." I look down at the woman in my arms and then out to the hall. To my bedchambers. Knowing this is a dangerous game I'm playing. "You can have Isabella, Galen. I won't fight you."

My brothers stare at me as though I've gone mad, but Galen is pleased by my words. Cyrus looks between us, before asking, "Drago?"

I stare back at him, waiting impatiently. "What?"

"You won't hurt her. Promise me." I'm shocked at his words. I know I must look as though I've gone mad. The woman is quietly sobbing in my arms as it dawns on her that the fight is useless. I look down at her and then back at my brothers, feeling selfish and undeserving.

"Never." I breathe the word and quickly turn to leave the room. I won't hurt her. I kiss her hair and stride quickly toward my bedchambers. I won't hurt her, but I won't let her go.

CHAPTER 2

GALEN

"WHAT THE HELL WAS THAT ABOUT?" Cyrus's question echoes exactly what I'm thinking. I purse my lips and watch Adelle lead the young women out of the room. Irritation rises inside of me as the shock of Drago's actions subsides. I'll figure out what he's hiding; there are no secrets in this castle that evade me.

"Why would he accept that offer?"

I ignore Cyrus's murmured thought. "Why would you let the sorcerer leave?"

My brother turns to me, a crease between his brow, and he answers, "You told him to. We don't contradict one another." Cyrus stares at me with his forehead pinched in confusion. "To be honest, I'm still shocked you allowed him to go." He runs a hand through his hair in exasperation.

"I shouldn't have." I shake my head, pissed at myself for not thinking clearly. "It wasn't wise."

"No it wasn't." Again, he stares toward the now

closed doors. "He's going to tell everyone what happened. They'll know it to be true."

I nod my head in agreement with his statement. "But we did not agree to war."

"We may as well have," he states matter of factly. With a heavy inhale he rises and I follow. We walk out of the throne room, and I smirk as we both walk toward the study.

"Are you intending on looking her up as well?" I have to ask him.

He raises a brow and smirks. "I'm not competing for her affection, if that's what you mean."

"It's not." Although a deep part of me is grateful for him bowing out, that wasn't what I was getting at. "Do you think she really exists? A woman who could carry our line?"

He shrugs his shoulders. "I haven't thought much of it." He looks away as he speaks, and I've learned that means he's lying.

"You haven't thought at all about having a mate?" My question is laced with doubt.

"Why would I? Our kind died out long ago, and the possibility of another species carrying dragonlings is"— he breathes heavily—"impossible."

I admonish him. "That's a strong word, Cyrus."

"It is the truth. It's best to accept it and live life to the fullest."

"To the fullest? As in constantly having a new woman in your bed?"

He scoffs at me. "No, that's not what I meant."

"Ah I see." No, I don't. I don't understand how one could live life to the fullest without a mate. I've wanted one for as long as I can remember. I thought I had her once, and my chest aches in memory.

"You're thinking of her, aren't you?"

I peek at my brother with a side-eye and nod. We know each other too well to hide from my brothers.

"She would have made you a wonderful mate. I liked her very much." Before I can read too much into his words he adds, "for you. She would've been good for you."

A familiar ache and pain flow through me, proving I'm not as numb to the past as I thought I was.

"I agree. But she's gone." It hurts to say the words. I think back to my sweet, innocent Kiera. I should have made her my mate as soon as I was able. We were so young though. Neither of us had truly learned to live yet. I remember kissing her in the towers. She'd pull away and smile shyly when things were just getting good. A small smile appears on my lips. If only I could turn back time, I'd never let her leave me. I would have loved her with everything I had.

"There's no use in regret." Cyrus's normally playful tone is gone. His hard voice breaks the happiness of my memory. "They're all gone and they're never coming back."

"When did you become the serious, cynical one?"

He huffs a laugh, "You were the one getting all glassy-eyed."

"You don't know what it's like to have loved and lost."

"Sure I do. Just as well as you." A grim look passes

quickly over his face. I know he's thinking about the purge. About the betrayal. My blood runs slow and cold as the memory consumes me. I remember the screams, and our mother locking us in the room. I'll never forget how the door shook and how Drago stood in front of us, prepared and fearless and ready to fight them off. That day we united as we were meant to. The day greed nearly brought an end to our species. "You may have another one to love if this woman Victor speaks of actually exists."

I'm grateful for Cyrus's words as they bring me back to the present. I snort in response and push the doors to the study open. "Let's find out who this Isabella is. I'm sure our scouts know something."

"What about Drago?"

"What about him?" My dragon rises and paces, daring him to question my claim to Isabella.

"What is with you two? So fucking possessive all of a sudden." He shakes his head with a smirk. "What the hell happened back there with Drago and that girl?"

I relax my shoulders and my dragon settles. "I have no idea. It's been a long time since he's shown any interest."

"That was more than simple interest. I wonder what it is about her that caused him to take her and run like that." I take my seat, worn leather that holds both comfort and memories at the desk, and type in my password as Cyrus takes his seat across from me. His expression is one of contemplation. "She doesn't look familiar to me. Do you recognize her?"

I shake my head with a frown. "I've never seen her before."

"Well, what the hell does he want with her?"

"I can only imagine one thing." Even as the words leave my mouth, I question them. He hasn't taken a woman in years that I know of. My finger taps against the keyboard aimlessly as I consider Drago's motive. "Perhaps he's fond of her. Maybe she reminds him of someone." I think back to Kiera. If I'd found someone who reminded me of her, I'd hold on as tight as I could.

"I don't buy it."

I quirk a brow at him. "Why don't you go ask then?"

A smile slowly forms on his face as he rises. The seat he'd taken no doubt still cold. "You know, I think I will."

My brow cocks as his wheels turn and he paces around the desk. His hand comes down on the back of my chair and he leans forward. "But first, let's talk to our contacts at the Authority and see who this Isabella is."

My thoughts are almost spoken, but I swallow them down. I hope she exists. I've wanted for so long to feel a connection with someone. Even if she doesn't love me back, I'll at least have our children. She will grow to love me, I'm sure.

I do my damndest to bury the hope deep down. It hurts worse and worse each time I've tried to bond and mate. But I can't help it blooming in my chest with a fire that will never go out. I want her to exist. I need to cling to the possibility of this Isabella being my mate.

CHAPTER 3

WITH A DEEP STEADYING BREATH THAT'S barely contained, I carry her down the hall, calming myself and my dragon.

I have her.

I have her to myself.

That's all that matters.

She's still in my grasp, but I'm all too aware she's on edge and filled with contempt.

It's a difficult task to open the door to my bedchamber with my little treasure in my arms. The moment I loosen my grip she struggles against me and kicks hard against my thigh. My hackles raise as I resist every urge inside me. Her kicks don't hurt me. There's no way she could ever harm me, but she does shove her weight against me enough to slip out of my grasp. Her small, frail body lands hard on the floor. A small whimper escapes her as her shoulder slams against the marble. Her face reflects the pain as she winces and sucks in air through her clenched teeth.

I despise that she's trying to get away from me, but

even more that she's hurt herself in the process. Her palms press against the hard floor as she tries to rise. I quickly snatch her small waist and hold her to me as I unlock the door and throw it open. She barely fights against me as I close the door and lock it, a habit I've had since we were younger. She writhes against me, and as much as I hate it, the fact that she's mine, in my chambers, eases any doubt. I will have her. She will have me. It's only a matter of time.

In the silence, she fights, but it's useless. I don't have to tell her so; all I have to do is wait a moment. She appears defeated as she cries in my arms. My dragon hates her pain. He claws inside me with a need to comfort her. I do my best to soothe them both, holding her tightly to me so she cannot fight before quickly laying her down on my bed. She scrambles slightly, eyeing me and then stiffening in a defensive position. The bed groans in protest as I sit next to her, but she scurries to the other side as quickly as she can.

Adrenaline races through me, and again I have to contain myself.

The bedroom is dark with the blood-red, velvet curtains covering the floor-to-ceiling windows. The windows are large enough that my dragon could break free of this room if need be. With the curtains closed, it's too dark to make out much of the room. I rise from the bed and let a flame blow up my throat and out to light the embers on a shallow, stone shelf that travels along the length of the room. The flames grow in both directions as they slowly bathe the room in soft light. The flames are only a foot or so tall, but the intimidating effect is undeniable.

Given the gasp that comes from behind me, she's never seen anything like what I've just done. My lips pull in an asymmetric smile, but I resist sharing that with her.

I center and contain myself before turning to face her.

The antique carvings in the stone walls of my family's crest are the first detail to come forward. The shadows and flames give the symbol of my heritage the pride it deserves. It's been ages since I've lit the room, and the sight of the emblem makes me wish I hadn't grown complacent with the dark. My large bed is draped with fine, gray silk fabrics, offering a canopy of shelter. The sheets and blankets themselves are a mix of grays and blacks woven together by the best seamstresses with the softest of materials. Several large pillows sit tall at the back of the bed. Although I've never thought much of it before, it's a sight of masculinity and wealth and my only comfort apart from my brothers.

As the fire lights the antique furniture in the room, I focus on the small, brave woman at the head of my bed. Her lips are parted in awe as she watches the walls slowly light. Her cheeks are tear stained and her chest is flushed from her struggle. I take the moment to look at her shoulder. The wound isn't as deep as I thought. She will need to be bathed, but the cut should heal well with a little touch of heat. I won't need to call a healer.

More concerning than the gash is the lack of fat on her body. The scant linen dress she wears is slashed from the whip, and her ribs and spine are easily made out. Anger threatens to consume me, and I resist once more, barely able to contain my dragon.

I will bathe her first and then she will eat. Everything else will be taken care of with time. Carefully and quickly, I round the bed and as I do, the fire cracks, stealing her attention and allowing me to get to her.

I wrap my hands around her waist, taking her attention from the fire and startling her.

"Let go of me!" She turns violently in my grasp and pushes away from me. Her efforts are futile. I ignore the agony her rejection causes. She knows not what she does. She knows nothing at all.

"Hush; there's no need to yell at me. I have no intention to harm you." With a trembling lip, she stops fighting and sticks her chin out. As if I cannot smell her fear. As if she could possibly control me. As if she has any authority whatsoever. She makes her demand. "Then let me go."

I have to repress my chuckle at her defiant command. I do not take orders from anyone. She won't be any exception.

"I'd rather not." A quick sob erupts from her lips and her fists clench in response. She turns her face away from me as I lift her and take her to the bath. "I'd just like to keep you company until you are well."

Even with the fear evident, she holds onto her anger, taking me by surprise.

"So I can be your whore." Her words are hard and drip with disgust. Her small body is shaking with fear even though her voice is strong.

My blood heats with a touch of fear. I want desperately to breed with her, but I have no desire to make her feel as though she's merely a toy to be used for my amusement. I hesitate, taking in this beautiful, defiant, yet beaten down woman, debating the best response. One that will let her know I'm attracted to her, that she would be my mate not a whore. But without her consent or desire to be with me, I struggle to find the correct words. I've never had a woman deny me, but this situation is a delicate matter.

"I do not want you to be a whore. Not for me or anyone else here." Doubt is etched into her beautiful eyes. But also, a hint of hope.

"You will come with me," I tell her firmly as I snatch her up again, holding her closely so she cannot fight. This time, she doesn't try to push me away.

I gently place her on the wooden bench and turn the tap to fill the bath. I kneel next to her, and I place my hand under the flowing hot water, reveling in the feel. I look at her pale, thin skin and wonder if the water would be too hot. I've never cared for another, let alone a human. I take her small hand in mine and grip it tightly as she tries to pull away. I give her a stern look, but her insolence is all I get in return.

"I'd like to know how the heat suits you."

She pulls her hand from mine and stares into my

eyes, warring with me, daring me to fight her. I only have to wait. After a moment, she slowly turns to the running water and lets it flow down her fingers. Her eyes close and a small sigh of wanting leaves her lips. My dragon purrs in my chest, loving the bit of happiness we've given her. "Is it to your liking?"

My lowly spoken question shatters the image of her content. She rips her hand away while nodding. Silence fills the room as she stares at the bottom of the large, soak-in tub, watching it fill. I truly despise the fact that she isn't giving me the respect she should be. She's obviously unwell and has been through hell with Victor. Rage boils inside of me just thinking his name. I'll rip his throat out the next time I see him. If I hadn't been so consumed with her, I would have ended his life before Galen had a chance to tell him to leave.

I'll let her anger at me pass with a warning and keep my tone soft and gentle. My intent is to charm her, to lure her in, but I can't set a precedence of her treating me disrespectfully. As she refuses to even spare me a glance, with the water filling the basin and steaming, I'm ever conscious of her state of mind. It's a difficult line to toe. "I expect you to look at me when I ask you a question." I do my best to speak calmly and not allow my anger or disappointment to show through.

Her eyes fly to mine but her lips remain closed. I wait a moment for her to acknowledge my words, but she fails to do so. "Do you understand?" She nods slightly, maintaining eye contact, but she doesn't give a verbal response. I don't care for that either. A fire rumbles in my chest. "I'd like you to answer me as well." Her eyes widen and her nostrils flare. "You may call me Drago."

She focuses her attention back to the tub making my anger flare. I repress it once again. "What name do you go by?"

"Kara." She whispers her name and puts her small hand into the bath, getting to her knees so her fingertips can glide along the surface of the water. The sight of her bent over hardens my dick. I push down my groan. She swallows and looks back at me over her shoulder. Her anger seems to dissipate. *Good.* I can't take much more of her resentment.

Kara. What a fitting, beautiful name for her. I love it. I love the way it rolls off my tongue. The sweetness of its whisper, yet strong in its demand.

"I'd like you to tell me about yourself, Kara." Her eyes look longingly into the bath and then back at me, no doubt wondering if I'll be here as she washes herself. And I will be. She threatened to kill herself only moments ago. There's no way I'm leaving her alone. Not only that, the cut along her back needs to be washed properly. I stand, opening the cabinet for appropriate oils, waiting for her to speak. Violet will help the pain. I grab the oil for the bath and continue talking to her. *To Kara.* My blood heats and my dragon stirs. I must be ever so careful with her.

As I shut the cabinet, our gazes lock. There's a crack in the tension. *Does she feel it too?*

She murmurs, still on her knees beside the tub. "What do you want to know?"

"Take your dress off." Her body stiffens at my request. I narrow my eyes at her. "I need to take care of your wound."

She stares back with trepidation. "You don't. I can take care of myself."

"We have a little dilemma, Kara." Her heart pounds in her chest so loudly I can hear every beat even though she tries to appear calm and strong. "I've decided I'd like to keep you for a while." Her face hardens with anger. "I'd just like to get to know you and care for you while you recover from everything you've been through."

She smirks at me and tilts her head. "I highly doubt that." I can smell her fear, but she stares daggers at me with courage. *I fucking love it.* I love her courage. But I need her to give me this. I can't have her hating me when I've done nothing to her.

"You can doubt it all you like, but that's not the dilemma. My brothers will be curious and I'd rather they not be involved with our relationship." I reach down and snatch the bit of fabric that's frayed and rip it off her body. It tears far too easily, jostling her as she fights to hold onto it. She's unsuccessful, and she gasps and quickly tries to cover herself. That's fine, for now. I turn sideways as a compromise. "In the water, Kara."

"Fuck you!" she practically hisses.

"You don't have to fight me on everything." I keep my eyes on the wall even though I badly need to gaze upon her body. I need to know exactly what state she's in. She's malnourished, but I'm hopeful there is nothing I cannot tend to. A long moment of silence passes, and I can just barely make out her movements in my periphery. When I see her lift her leg to sink into the tub, a heavy breath I didn't even know I was holding leaves me. The sound of her sinking into the tub tempts me to turn, but I resist until she's settled. Thank fuck. I don't know what I would've done if she didn't drop her resistance. I hear her hiss as the water hits the wound. The sound of her pain makes my heart clench and I lean down and let a few drops of oil drip into the tub before turning off the water.

"This will help with the pain." I dip the sponge into the bath and gently wipe the grime off her stiff shoulders. Her arms are crossed over her knees that are pulled up to her chest. "Does this feel all right?" I'm only grateful her fight has waned.

It takes her far too long to answer, her breathing is labored, and a small fear takes over my body, stopping my movements. "It's not making the pain worse, is it?"

She shakes her head. "No."

"Does it feel any better?" With her eyes closed, she slowly nods her head and whispers, "Yes."

Turmoil consumes me as I continue washing her back. My heart breaks for her. My poor, little treasure.

She needs time to adjust. I don't have time though. If my brothers find her... A thought hits me that chills my bones. I'd kill them for her. If they tried to take her from me, I'd fight to the death for her. The absolution in my thought is sobering.

The possession I feel for her is crazed. This intense desire to protect her, to have her, to kill for her affections. With the heady realization, I place the sponge in her hand and look away. I cannot allow these thoughts to be so consuming. It's far too dangerous. My tone is colder, "Wash yourself. Your back is clean."

The calming sounds of water soothe the bothered bits of my mind. As I stare ahead at the wall, centering myself once again and ignoring the pacing of my dragon, I focus on logical thought.

"As I was saying," I start and she pauses her ministrations for only a moment and then I continue, "my brothers will be curious about our relationship."

"We don't have a relationship."

"Not yet we don't. But we may, if we find that we suit one another."

"Suit one another for what kind of relationship?" She speaks her truth in a deadened tone. "A prisoner and her warden? Or worse?" I don't care for her response. But I also don't miss how it's validated by the events leading up to this point.

"You are not well. You're thin and obviously mistreated." I'm a fucking liar for saying this, but it's partly true. "I only wish to heal you."

"I don't understand why you'd want to keep that from your brothers." Her wit was not expected.

"Not just my brothers…" I grasp at anything to offer her a reason. "I don't desire to appear weak."

"You think it's weak to help others?" With her staring at me, waiting for an answer, I turn to face her, eye to eye.

"I think it can be perceived as weak and often taken as a vulnerability. But no, it is not weak to help others." She seems to accept my response. Her features soften and I can practically see her walls crumble. Good. That will help soften the blow. "Instead, I'm going to tell them you're my pet."

"Fuck you." She spits the words at me and backs away from me, splashing water with the violent movement. She pulls her arms out of the water to shield herself. It's as if she expects me to be aggressive. I'm reminded how little she knows.

"It's not as bad as it seems; Galen used the term some time ago. That's the only reason I call it that."

"It means I'd be your whore! I'd rather you beat me."

"It doesn't mean that at all. It means that you will obey me in front of them and I will reward you. I'll give you anything and everything you could possibly want. All I need is for you to do as I say."

"All I want is my freedom."

"I'm not letting you go." The response leaves me with the possessiveness I cannot control or hide.

"Then I'll simply starve myself." Her answer only angers me. Fuck her insolence. She will learn to obey me.

"You will not! If we are incompatible, then I will let you leave." I hate myself for giving her an out. And I'm not yet sure if I'll let her go when the time comes. But if she doesn't heat for me and she doesn't want me, then there's no reason to force her to stay here. With reluctance I add, "You have my word."

"You'll let me leave if I want to?"

"After you've regained your health, I will." I push down the fear of her leaving me. "If you don't want to stay, you're welcome to leave."

She seems to relax slightly as she registers my words. Enough at least to return to her bath.

I look away and grab a heated towel to wrap her in once she's finished. My heart is racing, and my dragon is pacing with the thought of her leaving. But I have time. I have plenty of time to let her adjust to the idea of being my mate. I'll make sure she's happy. I'll give her everything I have if she's able to give me dragonlings. I take in a deep breath and scent the air. Her heat is still prominent. She grabs the towel from my hand and the movement distracts me from my thoughts. She rises and covers herself, wrapping the towel and fastening it around her.

"Your brothers won't hurt me?" she questions.

"No. Never."

Thoughts riddle through her eyes. "Speak," I demand.

She crosses and uncrosses her arms. "What do you mean exactly by me being your pet?"

My dick hardens at the idea. It only occurred to me as a means to cover up the fact that she's a potential mate, but now I picture her, on her knees with those wide eyes on mine, wanting me to command her.

I'll be patient.

I'll earn her trust.

I'll earn her affection.

She will desire me. She will heat for me. She will be my mate.

CHAPTER 4

SHOVING DOWN EVERY DESIRE INSIDE OF ME, I stare back at this beautiful woman with wide curious eyes asking me what it would be like to be my pet.

Reluctantly, she takes my hand when I offer it to help her up from the deep bath. Her small hand in mine is like fire. It blisters through me with a spark that refuses to be denied. She's quick to wrap the towel around herself and leave me without her touch.

With a blush rising to her cheeks and her gaze anywhere but on me, I'm uncertain if she feels it too.

"You haven't answered," she whispers and then clears her throat. "What would it mean for me…to be your pet?"

I don't need magic to know she's thinking through every possibility. Her life has exchanged hands time and time again, more than likely each one worse than the last.

A possessiveness takes over so much so, a fire burns in my throat, deep and low and eager to meet my new enemies: anyone who's ever done her wrong.

"If I went along with it…with what it is that you want…" she murmurs and peers up at me through her thick lashes. Her natural beauty is undeniable, her shyness yet bravery enraptures me; there is no doubt that I would do a number of sinful things without mercy simply to please her in the hopes that she would do the same for me.

"What do you think it means?" For the first time, alone with this woman, I don't entirely trust myself. The color in her complexion deepens and her chest rises and falls as her breathing turns heavier. Again, she tries to hide it from me. As if I, a shifter, couldn't tell there's been a change. The heady scent of her desire is all I can focus on. It takes me a moment to hide away every thought that bombards me as she refuses to look me in the eyes.

"You want to sleep with me?" Finally her gaze meets mine, her long damp hair accentuating the curve of her neck, her body wrapped in only a woven cotton towel.

Her expression wavers. No matter how much she tries to hide it, she's terrified. Perhaps a mix of hopeful, resistant, wanting even, but I'm all too aware of the fear that lingers.

I'm ever so careful with my honesty. "I do…I very much do, but I don't imagine that would be best at this particular moment."

She's silent, her lips parted and so many questions riddled in her gaze.

I continue, ignoring the very present need that hardens at the thought of those lips parting for my cock.

"You've been through a lot already today," I say absently, to remind not only her but also myself.

"I've been through a lot on other days as well," she murmurs, the stubbornness and courageousness refusing to diminish as she dries herself.

"We could think of it as a game…" I offer and her motions pause.

"You possess obvious strength and I have respect for your bravery. But, as my pet, it is required that you submit in all ways." Her eyes flash with anger nearly instantly until I add, "In front of everyone else. In return, I will reward you with treasures beyond your wildest imagination."

She swallows thickly and nearly asks me something, but she swallows it instead.

"Submit…how?"

"I want you to submit to me and trust that I will do what's best for us. That's what a submissive would do." I add on for good measure, "It's important that they see this relationship that way. But you'll need practice first before I can let you out of my bedchambers." *Once her heat has waned.* I won't risk them scenting her. But once the heat has passed, I want her to meet them. "You won't have a problem obeying me, will you?" The very thought nearly brings me to my knees. Never have I wanted anything more than her submission.

"When I'm in front of your brothers, I'll keep my mouth closed and bide my time…" Her voice lowers as she agrees, "I'll do what you ask." My heart sinks at her intentions. I don't want her to *bide her time*. I want her to get to know me and see a side of me that few get to enjoy. I'd love for my little treasure to submit to me, to trust me, to want to please me. And fuck do I want to punish her and reward her, trust her and please her. I lick my lips, wondering what she tastes like.

"Being submissive is something that's learned." And she fucking needs lessons, that's for sure.

Her eyes narrow. "So I'll always be your submissive."

The rough pad of my thumb rounds the side of my fingers as I contemplate a deal that she won't refuse.

"When I call you my 'little treasure' that means we're playing. We can turn this off and on."

"So what do I call you if I want to stop playing?" she questions and a nervousness riddles its way through me.

"Nothing. A sub is always available for her Dom." Her eyes go wide with indignation.

"That's not fair," she tells me, her gaze striking through me, as if attempting to read my intention.

"I don't play fair." I move into her space, and with a hesitant step backward, she finds herself with her back against the wall. "I promise you that I'd never do anything to hurt you." She looks at me with disbelief. "Not physically or emotionally."

"Then how would you punish me? When I disobey?" I grin at her wording. *When* she disobeys, not if.

"Lack of reward my little treasure. I will ensure you are satisfied in every way imaginable, but if you displease me, you will be punished." I watch her shift her weight as a heat travels up her chest. My words turn her on. I scent the air and smell her arousal even heavier than a moment ago. The lingering steam from the hot bath carries the sweet aroma and begs me to satisfy her. A low grumble is buried inside of my chest and the dragon inside of me stirs. I fucking need this. *I need her.*

"What kind of things would you want me, no,"—she bravely stares back at me as she corrects herself—"tell me to do?" Her voice is on edge, and I know she's wondering if I plan on fucking her. And I do. I desperately need to fuck her and feel her come on my dick.

I sidestep her question, knowing I could so easily break this woman. She is fragile, vulnerable, and my needs will come last. "Whatever I do, or ask you to do, will only ensure your safety and I promise you we will both enjoy it."

"So, if I don't like it..."

"There are plenty of wishes you may not like and you can tell me so, but that may not change what I ask of you. You may not understand at first. You need to trust me."

"But what if I'm not good at what you want? What if I'm bad at listening?"

"Something tells me you'll be a fast learner." I take a step back, giving her distance and watching her body language. She wants this; she's just nervous. As she should be. "But I won't push when it's not necessary. Your feelings and needs will always be the first things I consider."

"What kinds of things will you have me do?" As she takes a step closer to me, she parts her lips. I'm all too aware beneath that towel is her bare skin. Her body is no longer tense. She's far more relaxed. That makes my dragon at ease.

"Whatever I desire," I answer honestly.

She hesitantly answers with a gentle nod and then she swallows thickly. She's hot and cold, exhausted from fighting but too on edge to simply be taken care of. I can feel it in the core of my soul. She wants to give in. She maybe even needs to give in.

"Now tell me a word, something that means I'm pushing a little too much."

"Pushing a little too much?" she questions.

"Yes." I rise and lean close to her as I kiss the crook of her neck. Testing her. As I expected, she stills. "Say I wanted to kiss down your body or fuck you on the floor. Not now, but once we've gotten to know one another." To my surprise, she clenches her thighs and arches her back slightly, ever so subtly.

"If I wanted to do that, Kara, at some point you may want to stop me. Or you may want me to be a little less rough with you." At the word "rough" she bites her lip and the smell of her arousal hits me immediately; I have to suppress my groan. *Fuck yes.* If she already wants me physically, this is going to be much easier than I anticipated. "If you wanted me to stop or to slow down, what would you say?"

My question breaks her lustful gaze. "I'd tell you to slow down or stop if that's what I wanted." I chuckle at her response. At least she's honest. I like that.

"My little treasure. I'm going to give you pleasure that will have you begging for me to stop. Not because you actually want it to end, but because you're afraid of how paralyzing the sensation will be. I will overwhelm your senses and take over every thought you have. And it will frighten you. Your initial reaction will be to make it stop. But trust me, you're going to want more."

"I'm not going to lie. That scares me." She shifts, unease rolling off her, so I decide to answer for her.

"You'll learn to trust me. And I won't ever push you too far. If you want me to slow down though, say yellow. If you want everything to stop, just say red. I'll immediately stop everything."

She cautiously stares back at me. I know I need to do something to prove to her that this is worthwhile. That she'll enjoy this. I run my thumb and finger down the sides of the cut on her back. "Like this." I stop my movements and wait for her beautiful hazel eyes to find mine. "I can make this pain go away. I want to."

"You can make it go away?" she whispers, and it's then I realize how much pain I can ease for her. She will find worth in me then.

"Yes. I can take it all away."

"How?" She's still weary, but at least she's willing.

"Come," I command her and move her how I wish. Her grip is white knuckled on the towel and her heart batters in her chest so loud I can hear it. When I tug the towel down enough to show the marks, she allows it. I pull her hips and position her body between my legs, with her back a few inches from my front. "Be still," I whisper at the shell of her ear, and I watch the goosebumps travel down her gorgeous skin. I let the fire burn in my chest and breathe it in and out. "When we're injured, dragons use the magic in their heat and fire to heal our cuts. You'll have to be very still." Her hips sway toward me as I breathe on her neck. My tongue flicks out along the gash, and I gently lick it. Healing it with my heated touch. I pull back slightly and kiss next to the wound. She leans in slightly to my touch, but then seems to realize her desire for more. She stiffens and I let her right herself, wondering more and more if she feels the attraction and need that I feel. If the heat affects her as it would a dragon mate.

My fingers hover over the small mark on her neck; it's looking better, but it'll take more than a single touch to heal her. "Did that feel good?"

She nods her head.

"I want to hear you, my little treasure."

"Yes," she answers nearly breathlessly. I love her obedience.

"Good." My eyes travel from her neck downward. I know she'll love my tongue on her pussy too. Not yet, but soon, I'll have her writhing under me. Daringly, I push her. "I want you to lay naked in my bed."

Her lips move to protest as she pulls away from me. I can see the hesitation, but she doesn't disappoint me. Instead, she squares her shoulders and nods slightly.

"Good girl. On your belly, so I can take care of your

wounds." Her shoulders sag slightly with relief as she moves to the bed, clinging to that towel although it hangs more loosely than before. I smirk at her back as she walks out of the bathroom, not waiting for me. Soon she'll be on her back with her legs around me as I pound into her. But she's going to have to earn it. And before that, I'll have to earn her trust.

CHAPTER 5

MY HEART BEATS OUT OF MY CHEST AS I LIE down on the bed, keeping my gaze on Drago. I do so ever so slowly and carefully. My gaze staying on his. Although my heart races and I can barely breathe, there's a calmness to everything that threatens the truth of what I know.

I'm surprised by how gentle Drago's touch has been. More so by how at peace I seem to be in his presence. I barely tense when he approaches, and it's been a long while since the sight of a man hasn't given me shivers.

This isn't what I expected. I don't understand any of it, not his treatment of me nor my response to him. Except for the fact that I am so very tired of fighting, and he's the opposite of what I've been told of dragons and what I know of shifters and supernaturals.

I've grown up watching those with powers torment humans for fun and take them as slaves or worse. Witches are especially horrid. Truth be told, I never thought I'd live very long. I can't even say I was surprised when I was taken. I was almost relieved that it would end sooner rather than later. Like my time had come and I no lon-ger had to wait around watching over my shoulder and not trusting a soul.

I hadn't anticipated living through it. I never thought I'd be at the mercy of someone who says they want to help me.

That cold shiver travels down my spine and my shoulders shudder at the thought. I don't trust him. I don't trust that he really wants to help me. My fore-head pinches, and I rub the line trying to ease the small headache radiating and growing at my temples. If he had wanted to hurt me, he would've done it by now. I bite the inside of my cheek. I just don't know how much to believe.

My reaction to him, the desire that overwhelms me, and the serenity that promises I can rest…it's proof enough he must've drugged me or cast a spell, or he's done something that has clouded my mind and judgment.

He is no hero. No one is ever coming to save me. That's a fact I've known for as long as I can remember. I do not believe a word he says and yet, I have to remind myself of that because my body begs to bow to his.

Drago doesn't give me a knight in shining armor vibe. Instead, he's a dark knight. The thought makes me close my eyes and try to repress a moan. Him ripping my dress off heats my blood in a way I've never experienced.

He's quiet as he heads back to the bathroom, his footsteps foreboding, and I steady my breath as I do what he said and simply lay here, in the comfort of luxury like I've never known. My eyes threaten to close and instantly the vision of his carved muscle in leather pants flashes before me. My eyes whip open and my heart races.

And oddly enough, there's disappointment when he's not here. The sound of him cleaning up in the bathroom tells me all I need to know, and I turn slightly and bury my head into the soft welcoming pillow.

It smells like him and I breathe it in deeply. Once again envisioning him.

It's like they're designed to seduce. Dominance and power exude from his dark, intense features. Yet his touch is soothing, and I find myself craving more.

I swallow thickly, reminding myself that they all lie. I need to be strong and keep my guard up. If he's working with Victor, then I need to get the hell out the first chance I get. Just the thought of Victor turns that heat of desire into ice. Anger simmers once again and that feels normal; it feels right. I'm disgusted that I feel the least bit attracted to someone who's willing to work with that vile prick.

"On your stomach." His low baritone voice rumbles with approval and I peer up to see his sharp silver gaze. It's nearly mesmerizing and the concoction of emotion is a drug that seeps into my blood. As I start to turn, his hand moves toward me but he stops himself and adds "No towel. I need to see you." My gaze shifts to a bottle in his hand and I imagine it's something for the wounds.

I slowly pull back the towel and expose myself to

him, embarrassment and fear return but I do as I'm told. My fingers graze my ribs and I instantly feel self-conscious. I haven't eaten in days—maybe two or three? I dare a glance up at him and his silver irises flash, it's enough to make me move as quickly as I can.

My body trembles slightly and I have to force myself to stop.

"It's all right my pet," he murmurs, and I brace myself for what's to come.

The fear and desire, the hope and the exhaustion, all combine as I close my eyes and wait.

"Once I've taken care of these, I'll go get you something to eat." He speaks evenly and lowly, just above his breath, as he hovers over my naked body. I moan into the bed just thinking about food and then stiffen as I feel his hands on my back. His palm presses lightly at the small of my back while the other moves my hair off my shoulders. My nipples pebble and my thighs clench slightly, adding to my embarrassment. My throat goes dry, and I can't close my eyes any longer as his heated touch slips down my spine.

He touches me as if he's exploring and my heart races all the while. A dragon. A real-life dragon. He lowers his head to the crook of my neck and whispers at the shell of my ear, "I'm going to take care of you."

I've never been so filled with want. His hot breath and the bite from the flames have a hint of pain as he licks down my back, but more than that it heats a low flame in my core. I bury my head and deny the feeling.

A deep rumble stirs in his chest and it's the sexiest fucking thing I've ever heard. Desire surges deep in my core.

As I contemplate what degrading things he must be planning for me, my body betrays me and arousal pools between my thighs. My cheeks flame with embarrassment, but he makes no acknowledgment of my body's reaction.

His hand travels lower as he takes long languid licks. His fingers move across the curve of my backside and down my inner thigh. The tips of his fingers are so close to my entrance. I almost curve my back, offering myself, and I have no idea who I've become. It takes everything in me to be still. To resist this man. To hell with my treacherous body.

Much to my disappointment, his hand travels farther down my leg as he pulls away from me. I immediately miss the heat. I've never been touched like this and the thought of him using me, I'm ashamed to say, it turns me on.

It's then when he pulls away that I realize these feelings I have at the moment are very much one-sided. His fingers travel down my back and along my spine. I know he's feeling how frail I am. I'm far too thin and weak.

"Who did this to you?"

I swallow thickly. "I did." His hand stills and then leaves me. A chill runs along my back.

"Why?"

It's difficult to speak as the memories come back to me, but I push words out. "It's a long story."

As the mattress dips with his weight, he huffs a humorless laugh. I half expect him to scold me, push for more, or to tell me how disappointed he is that I've ruined myself. Instead, he lays next to me and continues to kiss and lick my back, leaving trails of goosebumps as his heat leaves my sensitized skin. His touch is as if I'm lying in the sun. He is nothing but warmth and sunshine on the most beautiful of days. That's what it's like to be touched by him, and I find myself craving it until I realize it is only the magic that makes it feel so. It's not real.

My eyes open wider as I wish he could heal me without the need to be so physical. I turn my head to look at him, but his large hand comes down on my back and pushes me back down. "Stay. I'm not done." I do as I'm told, facing away from him and closing my mouth. Fine. I don't need to look at him anyway. It's probably better this way. "Now tell me why."

I should have known he would press. He doesn't strike me as a man who will allow privacy, even in the most vulnerable of ways. I swallow and breathe in deeply. "Because they wanted to drain me like they did the others."

His ministrations pause as he states more forcefully, "I don't understand. Start at the beginning."

The memories flash before me, and I hardly flinch this time. "The vampires took me. A few days ago, maybe a week." I lick my lips trying to remember, but the days blended while being locked in that dungeon. "I was with my friend, searching for our neighbors that'd gone missing."

I remember telling her it was a fool's errand, and she told me so was staying and waiting. Tears prick at the corners of my eyes. We both knew we were going to die either way. "It was just a matter of finding them. And we did."

"You must know that was a foolish thing to do." If I could laugh at the situation I would, but knowing what happened, any sense of humor evades me.

"Well it was that or wait around to be the next victim." There's a moment of tense silence before he kisses my neck, and I wonder for a moment if that was to heal a mark or simply to heal the unseen pain.

"I'm sorry."

"It's not your fault," I whisper and push down the lump growing in my throat. "They killed her and took me." His movements stop and he pulls my back into his hard chest.

"I'm sorry. I really am." He kisses my neck and his compassion nearly has me in tears. But there's no point in crying. I'll survive.

"It's not the first time someone's been taken from me by a vampire." He lays me back down on my belly and his hand runs soothing circles on my upper back where the whip landed only hours ago, yet I don't feel any pain. He leans lower and continues to heal my body. It's then I realize just how at ease my body feels. The pain slips away with his touch, and I'm filled with gratitude. "Thank you."

"Continue your story, my little treasure." I close my eyes, loving the name. As if I could possibly be something to treasure. I wish I didn't warm to his affection so quickly.

"Our town isn't protected, so I've gotten used to things…happening. People missing, or…" I don't finish the thought. I'm sure he understands. "We were planning to leave, as soon as we heard the protests and debates starting. But the process to be admitted into another town is long. It didn't happen in time."

"Where did they take you?"

"I don't know," I answer, hating the vision that flashes in front of me and wishing I could stop the memories or erase them altogether.

"Do you know why they took you?"

"To drain, like I said. They were taking blood from the humans to sell. Apparently using humans is efficient. We regenerate our blood fast enough to take what they need, then they come back and take again. Reusing us for their profits." I remember the cages, the leather straps that held us down and bit into our skin…the needles. It smelled like shit and blood. The thought has bile rising in my throat, but I push it down.

"They told me I was too thin to reuse so I'd need to eat more." I shrug my shoulders as if it wasn't the most horrific moment of my life, remembering how they tried to force me to eat. "Even when they put a tube down my throat, I was able to throw the food back up. I didn't want to live like that. I'll never let someone use me."

There's a long moment of silence and then he's no longer there; the warmth vanishes. The bed dips and groans as the insecurities run rampant through me and Drago climbs off the bed. I question my decision to tell him everything. It was foolish; what was I thinking? As the silence continues, I wonder if he no longer wants to keep me, to heal me like he said he did. I swallow thickly. It's fine if he doesn't, I tell myself. The thought makes my chest hurt and I'm not sure why. It'd be better if he didn't; I'd have my freedom.

"You're safe now." I turn slightly so I can see him and when he doesn't tell me to remain as I was, I turn fully over, covering myself with my arms as best as I can. He walks in front of me and leans down to move the hair from my face. "I'll take care of you." Maybe I should be ashamed that I'm skeptical that he'll take care of me, maybe I should be ashamed that I feel a slight reprieve from his statement.

I don't know anything anymore, let alone what I should think. All I know is that I'm exhausted and beyond my depths.

The light of the fire lining the walls of the room casts a shadow over his tall frame, making the deep lines of his muscles appear more rippled as he walks to an antique dresser. The sight of his bare back flexing as he opens the drawer makes me turn onto my side and face away from him. I can't take the fire he ignites deep in my core. My cheeks flame as I push the dirty thoughts away. I think of the teachings in school. The letters of the ancient languages. Anything to keep the thoughts of him on top of me, ravaging me, out of my head.

My body jolts as his large hand comes down on my shoulder, bringing me back to reality.

His hand stills and his tone is gentle when he says, "I didn't mean to frighten you. Wear this until I can find something more suitable." He places a large, button-down shirt next to me on the bed. Without hesitation, I grab the fine fabric and hold it tight to my chest, hiding me from his prying eyes. He gives me a tight smile and turns his gaze toward the door. "I'm going to get you something to eat."

I watch every move he makes and do my best to judge his thoughts and reactions, but I'm left with nothing other than insecurities I wish didn't exist.

As he nears the door, he takes a key out from just below the knob. I hadn't realized that he'd locked the door…and left the key in it.

That's odd. Surely he knows that I'd simply be able to unlock the door and leave. He sets the key on a small, dark, antique table and opens the door to leave. Then he looks back at me and back at the key, all the while strumming his fingers on the door frame. He cocks a raised brow in a humorous fashion that I didn't expect.

The humor forces my lips to twitch up, and once again there's a warmth I don't expect to feel and yet can't deny. I smirk at his back as he palms the key and pockets it on his way out. He's smart to take it; I have to admit I would be tempted to lock the door if given a chance.

Although it is just a door, and I am not naïve. The state of my predicament leaves me with a chill as I'm left alone in his bed. If I locked him out, I'm sure nothing would stop him from busting through the door. I take a moment to admire the intricate carvings that seem to shimmer with the low light from the flames.

A small shiver runs through my body, so I quickly put the shirt on. It's far too big, but at least it's something. I don't know what to think. A week ago, I was just me. A shit life in a shit town knowing more awful things were bound to happen. And then they did, and I fought it tooth and nail like I'd prepared to do. But now…

I just don't know how to react so I can survive this too. My stomach rumbles in pain and I curl into a ball on the bed. I was so stupid not to eat, but at least the vampires decided I wasn't worth the trouble and gave me away.

The sight of Drago on his throne flashes in my memory. I close my eyes and sigh as warmth flows through me. After a moment the chill returns and I cautiously pull back the covers. I sit cross-legged and stare at the door.

As if on cue, there's a knock. Every muscle tightens as I stare wide-eyed at the unlocked door. As a fear slips in that it could be someone else, the door opens and Drago enters. Only something feels off. I pull the covers closer to my body and up to my chest. He gives me a questioning look and tilts his head in an odd way.

My eyes travel along his body. I don't feel the same lust for him as I did only minutes ago. My back stiffens as he slowly walks toward the bed. His gait is different; something is wrong, and I don't feel anything I felt a moment ago. His lips part and then his eyes close as he inhales deeply. His hands land down hard on the post of the bed and his knuckles turn white as his fists clamp the carved wood frame. His grip is so strong I can only imagine he's going to destroy it.

My heart hammers and I struggle to speak. Something's happened and I don't know what.

I don't feel threatened by his actions, it's not threatening in the least. Although I can't imagine why he seems to be holding himself back from me. Maybe he's going to shift. The thought is as exhilarating as it is frightening. I've never seen a dragon, but I would love to. After a moment he seems to catch his breath and relax his grip, but he doesn't move. I don't understand. My brows furrow, and I swear he was wearing darker leather pants. I search his face again and notice a small scar I hadn't seen earlier. My breath freezes in my lungs.

This is not Drago.

The three brothers are nearly identical, but I know that whoever this is, it's not Drago. As if to prove me right, his eyes open and flash reptilian. But instead of the frightening red color I expect, his irises turn a bright green.

A fear like no other runs through me.

I kick against the mattress and push my body

backward until my shoulders slam into the headboard. Fuck, my head bashes against the hard frame. My heart races and all I can hear is his ragged breath and my blood rushing in my ears. My breath comes in pants as I stare back at him with wide, frightened eyes.

His eyes return to normal and his breathing calms. He slowly raises his hands in the air, palms toward me, and takes a step away. My muscles remain coiled though. I don't trust him whatsoever and I'm not ready to die.

"I apologize," his voice is calm and slow, but he speaks clearly. "I was not anticipating that."

My lips part but the words don't come. Swallowing thickly, I remind myself I cannot afford to appear weak. I will not be intimidated by him. I barely manage the question "Who are you?"

He swallows loud and harsh, the muscles in his throat tighten as he does. "Cyrus. I didn't mean to frighten you."

I nod in understanding and then I remember what he said. "Anticipate what?" Although my words are shaky, I'm proud I asked.

His mouth falls open, but he quickly slams it shut and shakes his head.

"I only came to speak to Drago. I didn't expect to find you here." *He's lying.* He saw me and didn't react like that at first. As I attempt to confront him, he blurts out, "I have to go." I watch with confusion as he turns on his heels and quickly opens the door. He looks back at me with a pained expression. "Don't tell Drago I came."

I have no idea what the hell is going on, but the idea of withholding from Drago makes my heart clench for some reason. He must sense my hesitation, so he adds, "Please?"

I'm flabbergasted by his request and his demeanor entirely, but I nod yet again, agreeing to keep this from Drago. He gives me a tight smile and leaves me perplexed, alone in Drago's bed.

CHAPTER 6

DRAGO

I CAN'T BELIEVE SHE DID THAT TO HERSELF, starving herself until her bones protrude.

Deep within my chest, my dragon snarls with the image of what they did to her. I'm all too aware that I need to know every detail of what's happened, though I can't stand that thought.

Breathing in heavily as I stalk the fire-lit halls, I nearly choke on the lump growing in my throat. The vision of her, and the idea of what would have become of my mate…it's indescribably horrific. The empty hall is silent apart from the crackling of fire within the torches. I'm only left with the visions of her and the idea of what she went through…what those bastards did to her. *To my mate.*

My jaw clenches as anger simmers and I take a moment. With my eyes closed and my hands clenched, I lean my knuckles against the stone, breathing in deeply. I need to calm the fuck down. They had her, my little treasure. They hurt her and used her. *They made her want to die.* The snarl that rips through me is uncontrollable and I roar with anger. My rage bellows down the hall as I slam my fist into the wall. The smooth marble splits and crumbles beneath the blow. The skin of my knuckles rips and blood drips down my forearm.

I merely flex my hand, staring at the crack and wishing I had the men who took her on their knees in the throne room. I'd let her watch as I burned them alive.

I can't change the past; it's a lesson my brothers and I have learned far too many times. However, I can kill Victor and anyone else who ever caused her pain. Leaning my neck to the side, I let it crack and tame my disdain, allowing my dragon to settle. I can put a stop to whatever the fuck they're doing. Victor may be right in that changes need to happen with the Authority, but I'm sure as fuck going to dictate what happens. Starting with the horrid events occurring in towns like Kara's.

Just thinking her name calms me. I focus on her needs in this moment and it pushes me forward. Her cut is healed and won't scar, but she needs to eat. I need to make up for the days she's lost.

The castle is nearly empty, and my footsteps fill the silence. I imagine at this late hour the servants are beyond our walls doing whatever it is that humans do, but there are always a few on hand for my brothers and myself at any given moment. I take long strides to the kitchen knowing someone will be there and I can figure out what to feed my little human.

I recognize the older woman stirring a large pot on the stove. The sight of her warms me a bit, calming the chaos that brews inside me. She's rather motherly to the others and has a sweetness about her that nearly reminds me of the way things used to be. I can't help but to be drawn to this woman as a child is to a mother.

The castle is ancient, but our kitchen is modern and massive. Nearly everything is for commercial use. It's essential. There are at least three families' worth of servants living here and we provide for all of them including ourselves. Dragons prefer red meat, as one would expect, although we dine on fine cuisine as well. I intend to spoil Kara with delicious and filling meals, but it's only then that I stop short, realizing I haven't the faintest idea of what my little treasure would order.

The woman looks up with a small smile that emphasizes the wrinkles around her pale blue eyes and mouth before setting the spoon down and turning to face me with her hands clasped in front of her while bowing her head slightly. "Lord Arrington."

A simper picks the corners of my lips up at her greeting.

"Adora, how are you this evening?"

"I'm well, my Lord. You have my sincerest gratitude for your gifts." It takes great effort not to stare blankly at her and instead I offer a tight smile and nod. Surely, that's Galen's doing.

"Certainly. I hope you've enjoyed them."

"They fit my granddaughter perfectly." I nod my head in understanding. A new birth. That makes sense although I wasn't aware there was an addition. Galen's fondness for company is not something we share. "What is it you'd like at this hour? I'll tend to it at once."

My eyes narrow slightly as I glance toward the cupboards. "I'm not sure," I admit and turn back to the human. "I'm in need of some information." Her lips part and her eyes go wide with trepidation. It's only then I realize she must imagine I'm here to question her about someone in the castle. It has been necessary before. I decide to quickly put her out of her misery. With a tight smile I confess, "I have no idea what it is humans enjoy eating and I'd like to provide for a guest." The old woman blinks rapidly as she takes in the information before relaxing her shoulders and offering me a smile. "I can certainly help you with that, my Lord."

"I'd appreciate it. I'd like to spoil my…" I hesitate to call her pet to the servants. I don't want them to perceive her in any way that would be less than my equal. After all, she may be my mate and mother to my children. She deserves the utmost respect. "My little human." Adora peers back at me with questions sparkling in her eyes but she knows better. No one here asks any questions.

"Spoil her with food?" she clarifies.

"Yes."

"This is the third girl? Not the two I'm currently cooking for?"

My jaw ticks slightly, noting she referred to my mate as merely a "girl", she is a woman and she is to be my mate. I grunt an agreeable response although my hackles are raised.

She nods her head and frowns slightly. "It's such a shame what happened to those poor girls," she confides in me, and I allow it for the moment. Only because it's her. Adora crosses the kitchen and opens the fridge as I follow behind. As she rummages and pulls out several packages, she tells me, "A lobster bisque is on the stove for the two now. I made sure to give them light food so they wouldn't get sick, but the bisque will fill them up."

I eye the pot although the lid covers the contents. "How long until it's ready?" I may be patient at times, but Kara lays in bed waiting for me and I do not intend to keep her waiting for long.

Adora turns to face me and shuts the door to the fridge with a nudge of her wide hips. Her linen apron hangs looser, showing her pale blue blouse as she arranges the items in a pleasant manner—a variety of cheeses, slices of plums and grapes, crackers and breads, and thin slices of meats. "It'll be another twenty minutes or so. But I'll bring it right up, my Lord."

"This seems fairly standard?" I question.

"It is." She nods her head respectfully.

"I'd like to spoil her; is there something more…appetizing to humans?"

Adora does something I've rarely seen, she cracks a smile. "Lord Arrington, I'm not sure I've ever told you how wonderful it is to live in the castle." My brows furrow in confusion until the woman continues. "Everything we eat is delicious. We have the finest of all sorts of meats and fruits we can imagine." Her eyes shine with wisdom and sincerity before she returns to the refrigerator. She pulls out a second silver tray that's already been prepared with a variety of olives and places it gently on the corner of the first. "I promise you she will enjoy *something* on this tray." I purse my lips and reluctantly consider taking the tray.

"When the soup is finished, I'll bring it to your chambers immediately."

I purse my lips again before asking, "What is the most delicious food?"

"Well, that varies from person to person, but I enjoy chocolate truffles." She smiles back with a knowing look. "They're a bit heavier for their state," she advises gently, "but I imagine a bite wouldn't hurt. I'll bring them up with your soup?"

I nod, understanding that perhaps a small but filling meal will be best for this evening. "Yes, I'm sure a bit of chocolate will be a nice finish as well."

"I assure you she will be delighted with the serving this evening," Adora states warmly, clasping her hands in front of her apron once again.

"Have someone bring the tray up."

"I will, my Lord."

With that I leave to return to my little treasure.

On my walk back to my bedchambers, I notice the light to the office trickling beneath the door frame. I'm uncertain if Cyrus or Galen occupies it, but I know I should check in with my brothers. They seemed concerned when I left with Kara, or rather when I stole her away unable to contain myself, and they should be. I silently curse myself for being so fucking obvious. Hopefully making an appearance and explaining my desire to have her as a pet will smooth things over. Steeling myself, I push the nerves down and prepare the tale I'll tell them.

"I didn't expect to see you so soon." Galen's tone is teasing as I open the door. "I didn't think you'd be able to pry yourself away." My brother sits at a common spot on the right and I make my way to him. I huff a laugh and look over his shoulder at the computer screen. *Isabella Faye.* The list of her heritage travels down the screen. It's impressive. There's no doubt in my mind she possesses the ability to breed dragonlings.

In the upper right corner lays a picture of the gorgeous woman. She has a pear-shaped body, beautiful brown eyes, and a bright smile. Her hair is lighter than Kara's, but nearly the same length, just past her shoulders. I expect to feel something, maybe jealousy, that I've given Galen his claim to her, but I feel nothing. I have my little treasure; I only hope she'll be able to carry my dragonlings. I'll know soon enough.

"I thought I should at least provide a meal for the distraught woman."

Galen's expression turns grim. "Yes, all three of them need to be fed well." He takes a heavy breath. "I wasn't thinking. I shouldn't have let Victor go without warning or consequence."

"We need to talk about that. It seems he's conspiring

with vampires. I'd rather they be less immortal and more…fucking dead. But not now. I want to get back to my pet."

"Pet?" He turns in his seat to look at me, and I make sure I keep my stare back even and carefree. I don't lie to my brothers, but for her, I'll make an exception.

"I can't help that I have urges of what I'd like to do to her, and I do believe she will enjoy it."

"You couldn't pick a more…submissive pet?" I huff a rough laugh at his question.

A broad smile grows on my face. "You have no idea how right you are to question that, brother." He smiles back at me and then turns back to the computer.

I tap his chair and turn to leave, but his voice stops me in my path. "I'm sure I still have my pet's collar somewhere." It's been years since Galen has kept a woman, but as dragons we tend to hold on to our keepsakes.

"No." The answer comes easily. "I want her to have her own."

A perplexed look crosses his face but only for a moment and then he busies himself again with the computer. *With his Isabella.*

In time, I'll buy Kara all the little trinkets a submissive should have. I'll get her a collar adorned with a small lock etched with my name: *Drago's treasure.* A grin pulls at my lips. I'll buy that first. In the silence I glance to where I expect my other brother to be, only to find his chair empty.

"Where's Cyrus?" I'm aware he doesn't appear to

be interested in this woman, but I'm certain he would at least be interested in researching her. He is, after all, always searching for something new and different to occupy him.

Galen looks back at me with a perplexed look. "He didn't send you here?"

"What do you mean?"

"He went to look for you." My blood chills at his words. "He's curious about the girl you took." Galen looks behind me as if she'd magically be there. "To be honest, I'm a bit curious as well."

I'm vaguely aware of the fact that Galen is still speaking, but I'm not listening to a damn thing as I turn my back on my brother, consumed with growing concern.

If Cyrus went to look for me, then he went to my bedchambers, which I left unlocked. He went to Kara. He's *curious* about my little treasure. My dragon breathes fire in my chest. I revel in the burn as it scorches my throat. Before I'm even conscious of my actions, my legs are pushing me through the opened study doors and down the hall.

He better not have fucking touched her.

CHAPTER 7

MY RAGE BOILS AND MY DRAGON FIGHTS against me as I stare at my closed door at the end of the hall. A possessiveness like I have never known consumes me. His talons dig into my chest, clawing to escape and go to our treasure. *Mine.* He snarls.

As I force him back, the fire burns up my throat. *Cyrus is in there with her.* I shove the door open so hard the wood bangs off the wall, startling my Kara. With wide eyes, she stares back at me from the head of my bed. My shirt, a crisp white button-down, is far oversized on her and makes her appear all the more fragile. She's rolled the sleeves up her forearms. Her damp hair has dried somewhat, and color has returned to her cheeks. Without trying, she's stunningly beautiful.

Her eyes widen even further, and she somehow manages to scoot back farther from me and press her back against the headboard. It's only then that I realize I have my fists clenched and I'm practically breathing fire. I slowly calm myself as I glance around the room.

A low growl stays buried beneath my chest as I search the room for any hint of Cyrus. He's not here, but he was. My nostrils flare; I can smell him. Lucky for both of them I can tell he didn't touch her. Or at least he didn't fuck her. With great effort, I relax my posture and look back to Kara. She shifts her weight under my stare and pulls her legs into her chest and under the shirt. Startled at the very least, she swallows thickly but maintains my gaze.

"I didn't touch anything, if that's what you're thinking." My lip pulls up at one side. *What a sweet little liar.*

"Tell me, treasure, what did you do then, while I was gone?"

"Nothing." She's far too quick to answer and her voice is a higher pitch than it's been with me.

Deceit is not a good look on her. The fire of the room crackles as I pace my way to her.

There's no way he came in here without her knowing. The question is: why is she keeping that information from me? She shakes her head calmly, but her heart races and I can easily hear it pounding.

I don't take my piercing gaze away from her gorgeous hazel eyes.

"Is there anything you'd like to tell me?" I offer her an out as the adrenaline rushes through me and the sickening feeling of being lied to washes over me.

"No." She swallows loudly and glances at the door that I left cracked before looking back at me. "Have you brought food? I'm hungry." Her request snaps me out of my predatory gaze.

Apparently keeping secrets from me has made her more submissive. I enjoy that. More so than anticipated. "If it's all right, I'd like to eat," she says as if eager for my approval and permission. Her eyes beg me to change the subject, and I know right then and there, Cyrus will answer for this. Not her; not my mate.

As if on cue, the door opens wider with a push of Adora's hip, she enters with the tray carefully held as the dainty china clicks with every small movement.

I meet her at the entrance, accepting the tray and placing it on the bed in front of Kara.

"Thank you, ma'am?" Kara scoots closer to the tray with her eyes on the older woman.

"Mrs. Adora, dear." Her voice is much softer and sweeter addressing Kara than she was with me. She carries a gentleness with her as she speaks, although her eyes widen, no doubt assuming a certain situation has occurred, given Kara's state.

Adora barely glances at me although the questions in her eyes are apparent. I'm quick to dismiss her. "Thank you. You may leave us now."

As soon as the door closes, Kara reaches for a square of cheese and I bark out the order to stop, a little too loud and a little too abrasive. With wide eyes she stares back at me, clearly taken aback.

"I merely wish to feed you myself."

Her shoulders relax with obvious relief, but it's short

lived as I climb into the bed beside her. Her heart races as it did before, but the moment I get close enough to feel the heat from her body, the scent of her arousal greets me. Her cheeks are flushed and her heart pounds with desire. I position myself with one leg off the bed and the other tucked under me. I'm close enough to feed her, to touch her, to kiss her. As my cock hardens, I attempt to control the tempting thoughts that ride through me.

Swallowing thickly, I dare to push just a little. I position myself in front of the tray and pat my lap. "Come sit, my little treasure." Her eyes go round as she looks from me to the tray, all the while that racing heart gives her away. After a moment, she very slowly obliges, settling her ass in my lap. Her warmth is electrifying. With her back to my front, desire stirs the flames deep within my chest. I can barely breathe as she steadies herself by placing her small hand on my thigh. I grab her waist and move her to the center. Her lush ass sits perfectly against my cock.

In a desperate effort to focus on her wellbeing, I snatch the square of cheese she wanted and bring it to her lips. Her hands move up to take it from mine. "Uh, uh." I shake my head and admonish her. "I want to feed you. I will give you all that you want." My voice is low, my tone giving away my desire. Her lips are parted slightly, and her eyes reflect rebellion as much as they do everything else she's feeling.

I stare back into her eyes, thinking about what a bastard I am. It would be all too easy to allow her peace and quiet, to ease her slowly into being my companion, rather than push her as I'm doing. Patience will award me riches, but so has thievery and fire.

After a moment Kara rests against my chest, plants her hands on my thighs, and opens her mouth wide enough for the morsel. As her lips part, her chest rises, and my eyes inadvertently catch a glimpse of her breasts. Want and need heat inside of me.

They're perky yet small with hardened rose-pink nipples pressing against the fabric. I stifle my groan and pray she can't feel my dick hardening beneath her. As I slip the piece of cheese into her waiting mouth, her eyes go wide and her back pulls away just slightly from me. Fuck, she definitely felt the change beneath her ass. She stills and slowly chews while looking straight ahead.

The intoxicating smell of her heat is laced with disappointment because it's far too obvious that she's terrified. It's dimming. She's already losing it. I choose to simply ignore all of it and grab another square of cheese to continue feeding her. "Open." She immediately obeys, and those pink, plump lips part for another bite. I smile as she closes her eyes and enjoys the taste.

"Do you like it?" She quickly nods and lets a small moan of gratitude slip into the air between us. Her eyes pop open and her hand covers her mouth as she realizes her action. Again, I choose to ignore the look of regret in her eyes. "Good." I reach for a slice of ripe plum. "Would you like to try this next?"

"Please, Lord Arrington." I stop my movements as

my eyes travel over her face. I don't know why, but I don't like her calling me that. She is not a guest, nor a servant. Something deep inside me whispers that she may only be a guest, she may leave me soon, but my dragon and I disagree. I want this to be different. Something about her calls to me. Galen had his pets call him Master, but I don't want that. I decide on something more to my taste.

"I'd rather you call me Sir."

"Yes, Sir." My dick jumps in my pants and her face flushes red. She looks down and bites her lip to hide a smile. What a little vixen. She knows exactly what she's doing.

I slip the sliver of fruit into her mouth. I repress my groan as her hot tongue licks the tip of my finger. A satisfied sigh fills the room. "You like that more?"

"I enjoy both." She looks up at me through her thick lashes. "Why are you being so nice to me?"

The question catches me off guard. I want to tell her about her heat, my desire for a mate and dragonlings, and how she is the only hope I have of such things… But I'd rather not, given I have no idea if we are truly mates. I settle on a simple truth. "Because I want to."

She takes a moment to consider my words. "Thank you. Could I have some more?"

"Of course."

Time passes easily, piece by piece. I continue to feed her, enjoying the feel of her warm body and the small sounds of satisfaction from her lips. Then I remember my brother and the fact that she's yet to tell me he was here.

"I have a question for you, treasure." I tilt the spoon up so she can taste the soup. She swallows with a sign of contentment. Her tongue darts between her lips and then she finally looks up at me.

"Yes?"

"Is there anything that you're deliberately hiding from me?" Her heart hammers against her chest as she looks back down at the tray of food. "Open treasure. You need to eat more." I want to make sure she knows she gets to eat regardless of punishment. I will never deprive her of necessities. She hesitantly opens her mouth for me to slip in a slice of sharp white cheddar. There's still some prosciutto and sweet salami left, as well as some kumquat jam and Marcona almonds. Plenty to slowly treat her, and test her, and flirt with her in this manner.

"Yes." I wait for her to continue, but she doesn't. She turns her head, refusing eye contact and concentrating on the dark comforter.

"I see," I say as I reach for a chocolate truffle and hold it up for her to eat. After all, she did answer my question with honesty. "Dessert treasure? Unless you're full."

Her eyes dart to mine with surprise. She accepts the chocolate and I give her another while asking, "What is it that you're keeping from me?"

"I was asked not to say." Her voice is sorrowful as she answers me.

"Hmmm." I press my lips together and pick up another chocolate, but she shakes her head and fiddles with her fingers in her lap. "Are you full?"

"Yes." A moment passes between us, and I take the break to settle her in the middle of the bed and move the tray to the dresser before returning to her. She brings the sheet to her lap as armor, as I war inside with how I should handle this.

I don't care for that fact that she's keeping things from me. And I especially don't like that I have to pry information from her only to be given short responses. However, the fact that she keeps her word is admirable.

After clearing my throat, I pry more. "Answer me this." I climb onto the bed and sit next to her, this time she doesn't shy away, but stays where she is. "Did anything happen that frightened you while I was gone?" I highly doubt Cyrus did, but I still need to ask. For an odd reason, the weight of the world seems to settle against me as I wait for her answer. I do not wish to kill my own brother.

She shakes her head and answers, "No." As relief slowly washes over me, she adds, "For a moment I was a bit scared, but everything was fine." I stare at her, wanting more, and then I realize the best possible solution.

"From now on, my treasure, if someone asks you to keep something from me, I want you to tell them that you can't." It's then she realizes I know at least something and a spark flashes in her eyes. I'm careful as I bring my hand up and brush her hair from her face.

"I wish to know everything about you and everything that happens to you. You will do that for me, and

I will ensure they understand that it is not prudent for you to keep secrets from me, is that understood?"

A shy smile plays at her lips. "I can do that, Sir."

Fuck. I love that she added that "Sir" for me. Even more so that she seems to be enjoying the game. I scent the air again and her heat has nearly vanished. She's still aroused, which is nice, but not what interested me in the first place. It's possible it will come again in a few weeks. I will keep her until then.

She yawns drowsily and quickly covers it with her hand. She truly is a beautiful creature.

"I need to reward your good behavior treasure." I watch her out of the corner of my eye as I climb off the bed toward the nightstand and blow a gentle flame onto the large wax candles throughout the room. Some are large pillars of wax a few feet high and the flame slowly grows nearly a foot tall. Others are smaller and sit atop the furniture. I walk the length of the room and light them until the room is lit with a warm glow. She watches with wide eyes as the flames slip from my lips effortlessly like a whisper of treacherous secrets.

"And then you can sleep."

"W-what is my reward?" Her voice is laced with apprehension.

I smirk at her and answer, "A touch of fire that only a dragon can give you, my little treasure." She swallows thickly while pulling her legs inward and wraps her arms around her knees. Her breathing becomes shallow as she stares at me, the fire echoed in her gorgeous eyes.

"Are you…" she whispers but doesn't finish. I can smell her fear.

"I'm not going to fuck you." Her breathing stills with my statement. "I don't think you're ready for that. Are you?" Her hazel eyes dance with uncertainty.

Shock overwhelms me. *Is she truly debating it?*

She may think she's ready, she may want physical affection, but not sex. Not yet. Not until she knows exactly what the consequences of that may be. I won't push, although my dragon is desperate for her.

"Then what is my reward?" she asks breathlessly.

I stare at the button-down shirt she's wearing; it's made of natural fibers, which is good. Anything else could melt or ignite. And I know she isn't wearing any perfumes or lotions since I bathed her myself. "Massage. It's therapeutic and I think it would do you some good." I make my way back to the nightstand and cock an arrogant brow. "Undress again and lay on your belly."

"Could I lay under the blanket?" Her hands are already at the buttons. Good girl. Who would've thought she'd be so eager to please me?

"Just your bottom half." *For now.* I climb on the bed and take a candle from the table as she lies just like I told her to. I tilt the candle and let the wax fall into my palm. It's primarily cocoa butter designed for such things, and I rub the liquid between my hands.

I knead her shoulders and neck as I ask, "Fire is a magical thing. Do you know some people worship fire?" Small moans escape her. I smile knowing she's enjoying herself as the tension melts away. "Dragons have been worshipped and loved for their ability to create a flame from nothing. We're feared just as much for the same reason." I straddle her upper thighs and move my hands down her back, massaging circles into her stiff muscles. "But few know what pleasure fire can give."

"Mmmm." I chuckle deep and low and wipe the residual wax off her back, continuing to rub and knead her tense body. My fingers graze along the flesh that was struck by the whip. No evidence remains.

Her body slowly relaxes under me. The moment sleep seems to tempt her, I stop, knowing she will thoroughly enjoy what I plan and will sleep far better when I'm through with her.

"Roll over treasure." I lift my ass off my heels and stand on my knees, still straddling her. She looks back with a weary glance before rolling and covering her breasts. Her bottom half is still covered by the blanket. I sit back on my heels and prepare for a bit of a demonstration. As soon as her eyes are on me, I breathe fire over my forearm, letting the flames lick and bite their way down my path. I quickly wipe the path with my other hand and hold it up for her to see.

Her eyes go wide and she gasps. "You hurt yourself!"

As the heat dances on my now sensitized skin, I chuckle rough and low again before answering her, "No my treasure, the feel of a flame is incomparable to any other touch, the soft lashes are meant to heighten pleasure."

Her lips part in shock as she asks, "Are you going to light me on fire?"

"Of course not. I don't want to hurt you. You should never be in pain. I just want to give you a pleasure only I can give." She looks unconvinced. "Hold out your arm." She hesitates but it doesn't take long for her to give me her right arm as she still covers her breasts with the other. "I'm a shifter." My words get her attention. "I don't mind your nudity."

I trail my fingers gently up and down her forearm and grin at the goosebumps my touch leaves behind. Before she can object, a low flame bellows from my chest. Gripping her wrist to keep her still, I run the fire down the inside of her forearm and watch it tickle her skin and extinguish itself. My other hand gently calms the skin as the flames die. I look back at her and find her lips parted and eyes half lidded. It's a look of awe and enlightenment. I know the endorphins must be rushing her system, heightening her arousal. They'll give her a greater sense of pleasure. Just the idea that fire play excites her makes my dick hard as steel. I ignore the fact that I could easily bury myself deep in her heat. But not yet. She's not nearly ready for it and she's been through far too much as it is.

I set her arm down gently on the bed and knead her shoulders. Her hair is in the way, so I lift it up and onto the bed, feeling her loose silky waves and reveling in the control she's given me. "Close your eyes and relax." Her hazel eyes look deep into mine with a look that tortures me—one of desire yet also distrust. I knead into her tense shoulders. Only once she's finally relaxed and lets her shoulders fall do I lean in. The crack of the fires burning around us fuels my own flame.

I kiss her skin with the bite of my flame, letting it dance across her collar bone before licking the sensitized skin. I pull back slightly to ensure the color is right. A healthy pink, exactly what I want to see. A soft moan pours from her lips as she clenches her thighs. I can smell the arousal pooling between her legs. I close my eyes and resist my own urges.

I do the same to the other side: massage, fire, kiss. My tongue travels languidly along her skin. I lick up her neck and continue to rub her tender skin, soothing it. I blow the flame along her exposed throat, keeping it low so she's safe from the dangers fire can bring. She writhes beneath me and moans the softest, sweetest sounds. I could easily rock onto her throbbing clit and get us both off. But I have to remind myself that I can't push her too quickly. I can't move us too fast. Only hours ago, she'd accused me of wanting her for sex; I don't want to give her any reason to believe that claim was justified. No matter how much I wish to thrust into her and fuck her into my bed as if she's always belonged to me.

My eyes travel along her now-flushed skin. Her nipples are hard, and the sight of her breasts makes me lick my lips. I can only imagine the sweet sounds she'd give me as I suck and nip her hardened peaks. Precum leaks from my dick, begging to be inside her. Her eyes are still closed and I doubt she's aware of how she's rocking herself against my leg. I lean down, ignoring my own needs by giving her clit more pressure that she'll need to get off. I gently place my hands on her sides and massage up toward her breasts. As I reach the first, I keep my eyes on her face, watching for her reaction. Her breath comes in fast pants and her head rocks side to side, but she makes no signs that she even notices when I begin to knead her breast.

I take her breast in my hand, it's the perfect fit, and squeeze gently. I allow it to slip out of my hand and gently tweak her nipple. I squeeze a little tighter, watching her expression. Her lips part in ecstasy and her back bows as I slowly pull on her. She gives me every sign I need to continue, but I want to remind her of her safe word. I need to know that she's with me on this.

"Treasure?" I ask.

"Mmm." Her own hands go to her breasts, and she begins kneading them and twisting her nipples. Perhaps she is still very much in the throes of her heat. I place my fingers over hers and squeeze them tight, pulling her nipples a little more than she was. A whimper of pleasure leaves her lips as her hardened peak slips from our grasp.

"What word do you need to say to make this stop?"

Her hands gently rub along her breasts and she keeps rocking into me as she whispers, "Red." I smile, although she can't see my reaction with her eyes closed.

"Good girl; and do you want me to kiss your breasts with fire?" I know she's close to her release. I can see her desperation. This would do it. This would give her exactly what she needs.

"Yes"—her back bows as she finishes—"please, Sir." I nearly reach my own orgasm just hearing her soft plea.

I lean down and take a nipple in my mouth to suckle and bite gently, pulling up and releasing her tender skin. I'm all too aware of how careful I must be on such sensitive flesh. I lick below, beneath the swell of her breast and travel upward, swirling my tongue and wetting the skin, before lighting it aflame. I lick behind the fire as it gently dies on her skin. She arches her back and cries out as waves of pleasure numb her skin. Her body trembles beneath me. My dick leaks more precum, begging to be inside her heat, but I ignore my own needs.

I pull the covers back and lay next to her as she comes down from her orgasm. I carefully cover her body with the blanket and pull her back to my chest to kiss her hair and tell her what a good girl she is.

My hard-as-fuck cock won't fucking die. With my hips angled back, I attempt to keep my condition from being noticed. I could go into the other room and take care of it myself, but I'd rather wait. A smile pulls at my lips as I kiss her hair again. The next time, I'll find my release with her. I'll feel her come on my cock. My dragon stirs inside of me as I inhale the scent in the air, and I'm met with a bit of disappointment. There's only a faint smell of her lingering heat. My chest seems to be crushed by an unseen weight. I truly desire this woman. I want her to be *my mate.* I need to remind myself that our time may be limited.

Her chest rises and falls heavily and chaotically as she comes down from her release. I can tell the very moment the endorphins leave her and she comes to her wits. Her body stiffens in my embrace and her breathing seems to halt. I keep my hold on her and roll onto my back. My dick aches and begs me for its release as it sticks straight up in the air. Fuck, even the feeling of the comforter could get me off. I close my eyes and push it down, and then pull and turn my sweet submissive so that she's laying against my chest. Her eyes dart to mine and then down to the obvious bulge beneath the comforter.

I wrap a strong arm around her and pull her small body closer to mine. She resists a little but comes to me. I don't like that she resisted so I feel the need to ask again, "What color to stop it, my treasure?"

Her eyes soften and she looks up at me through her thick lashes. "Red," she answers in a sweet voice. I lean down and kiss her hair again.

"That's right. Good girl." She slowly puts her full weight against my body and relaxes.

"Sleep now; you need your rest." I run my fingers along the dip in her waist and end my perusal of her there.

As she settles and seems to understand my intentions are to lay beside her and nothing more, sleep pulls her in.

As quietly as I can, I reach to the nightstand to pick up the tablet. Eager to distract myself.

With one hand I open it and start a search for what the internet will provide me with, but I haven't the faintest clue where to start other than "missing person named Kara." And that search doesn't turn up shit. I'll have to get everything I can from her in the morning. Somewhat disappointed, I decide to make a list for Sage, a housekeeper of sorts.

She'll pick up everything I need. I'll get Kara all the basic things she will need and everyday attire. It's rather boring and tedious so I keep the task for Sage. Then I shop for my treasure. I pick out a beautiful and intricate gold collar from a private jeweler I've known for decades. It's thin and appears delicate but made with an enchantment to ensure its strength. I look down at my Kara, eyes closed and seemingly in a deep peaceful sleep; it's perfect for her. The shadows that the fire casts trail down her delicate features.

It takes far too long for my attention to turn back to the task at hand.

I choose a few more items and a particularly appealing golden dress, if you can call the scrap of cloth that. Finally, I pick out another piece of jewelry that will be fun to play with. It's a long chain that will attach to her collar at one end and the other end will gently clamp her clit. A tug of the chain will give her more pleasure than she could ever imagine. A sarcastic smile grows as I turn off the tablet and run a hand down my face.

That did not do anything to help my erection.

I rest my head against the pillow. Today has turned out to be quite extraordinary. The only exception being the fact that my little treasure is merely pretending to sleep across my chest. Her breathing is uneven and occasionally her eyes move behind her lids. It's nearly comical how bad of a job she's doing.

I put a hand behind my head and get comfortable. I'll do a better job pretending how to sleep, then I can figure out what my treasure is up to.

CHAPTER 8

As I lay in the silence, my pounding heart gives me away. It's beating out of my fucking chest so loudly I'm certain it will wake Drago.

What the hell just happened?

With the heat lingering over every inch of my skin, all I can think is that his power or a spell or something else has taken over and demanded I desire him. If he'd asked me to part my legs for him, I would have without hesitation. I would've given my virginity to him without even thinking twice.

Swallowing thickly, I'm as still as can be with the steady yet faint rise and fall of his broad chest beside me. His scent and warmth wrap around me and confuse my thoughts. One is far too evident though: I'm in way over my head.

I know how to fight. I'm prepared to fight. But this? I'm not prepared for this. I've never even considered these desires and wanting *this* with someone. The passion. The desperate need to feel him and allow him to do whatever he'd like…this is a torture I've never known.

How could I possibly feel so strongly for someone I've only just met. *Fated mates. Love at first sight.* I've never believed in that shit. As Drago's position changes slightly and the bed groans along with his movement, I will my trembling body to stay still and try to keep my breathing from coming out ragged. I swallow, and the movement makes my chin bump against his hard, rippled chest. Simply having my skin meet his allows a fire to rage through me, and the memories of what just happened elicit an even stronger need.

When he licked me and heated my sensitized skin with his fire, all I wanted was for him to thrust into me. I felt as though I needed him. The ache is still yearning for him to take me. I've never been so open, so bared to someone. I completely let my guard down.

How fucking stupid could I be? It must be magic. I'm simply caught in a spell.

Drago takes a deep breath causing his chest to rise. His masculine scent fills my lungs, and the intoxicating lore tempts me to peer beneath the sheets. I'm certain he's still in need given the bulge that's impossible for him to hide. It takes every ounce of strength to remind myself that this isn't real.

But as the time passes ever so slowly, I can't keep myself from thinking about him. From wanting him.

I need to get the fuck out of here.

With the anxiousness riding through me to escape

before I lose myself entirely, I can't help but question if he's truly asleep. If it's that easy for a beast like him to simply give in to the night. The voice at the back of my mind begs me to be patient and not rash…or else. So I lie as still as I can, fighting the deep need to close my eyes. I try to remember the route we took to get here, to his room. But all I remember is screaming and kicking against him. When the escape plan devolves into nothing more than "run," I stare at his gentle sleeping form. My gaze travels down his sharp jaw to the dip in his throat and I wonder why he wants me. He could do this to anyone…why me?

He said he wants to heal me. But he already has. The pain has vanished.

I don't need anyone to help me. As a breeze bangs gently against the glass, my gaze flicks up to the iron paned windows. We're far too high up for me to escape. Thinking of leaving him, of being anywhere without him, sends a painful bolt through my chest. It's yet again another sign that I'm not well and not myself. I've never felt attached to anyone. Certainly he's using me as a play thing and manipulating me in order to make it easier for him. I could never love a man like that.

I realize I'm nodding my head at my thoughts and my eyes dart to Drago's. His chest rises and falls. I watch as my breath gently moves the hair on his chest. My fingers itch to run through the thin line of his happy trail. The covers are just barely at the dip of his hips. That sharp *v* makes my mouth water. I clench my thighs and shut my eyes tightly, hating the pull he has over me.

As carefully and quietly as I can, I gently lift my body off his. All the while I watch him. He's still. Asleep like the dead. With just the sight of him controlling me, the memory of his flames moves my fingertips to my neck. The feel of him is like nothing I've ever known. It's a drug, a spell…it's something deadly.

Moving as slowly as I can and wincing with every noise the mattress makes, I lift the covers and scoot off the bed. The chill in the room makes me extremely aware of my lack of dress. I can't very well sneak out of here naked. I bite my lip and look around the room for the shirt he gave me.

I get on my knees and search for it on the floor. It doesn't take long to find it and slip it on. As the soft scent of him wafts over me once more, a small smile plays at my lips, at least I'll have that to keep. There are no undergarments though. I fix the sleeves and decide this will do for now. With every small step to my escape there's a slight groan of the ancient wooden floor. Each time I peer back, the longing for him only intensifies. As if my very soul rages war against me for leaving him. I remind myself that all spells can be broken and perhaps space will aid me in that endeavor.

His door is locked with the key still sticking in the keyhole. I unlock it slowly and wince when the click that I've never fucking heard is the loudest fucking sound ever. My shoulders hunch and my breath comes to a halt.

I expect to hear something, but after a moment I take a peek over my shoulder. Drago is still sound asleep.

I let out the breath and gently open the door. It's relatively quiet, but I do it slowly to make sure the sound is at a minimum. Once it's open, I place the key on the little wooden table by the door and sneak out. I almost look back, but I'm afraid if I do, I won't have the courage to leave. As soon as I'm past, I gently shut the door, but I don't close it all the way. I don't want the sound to wake him.

As I take a few quiet steps into the hall, with only the sound of my bare feet smacking against the cold floor to accompany me, I realize I'm not even sure if I ever thanked him for healing me and for the meal I so desperately needed. With every step I feel more ungrateful and sorrowful. I shake my head at the thought and continue walking...this is not the thinking of a woman who is going to survive this. I focus on where the hell I am so I can figure out where I'm going. The walls and floor of the long hall are made of beautiful white and black swirled marble. Torches are lit along one wall, but most have gone out, leaving dark patches in my vision. Fear trickles into my blood as I pass through a section of darkness only to find a light shining through much brighter than the torches.

I hear the soft sound of women's voices as I approach a well-lit room. The door is cracked, causing it to send a stream of bright light onto the floor.

"Thank you so much." I hear a soft voice crack with gratitude. I think I recognize it, but I'm not sure.

"You really must stop thanking me." That voice, I'm certain, is Mrs. Adora's.

"I don't know how, but I promise I'll learn." I listen to the soft voice as I hold my breath and dart across the door, hoping they don't see me.

"Yes you will, and I will help you along the way." Mrs. Adora answers her with confidence, and I breathe in relief. They didn't see me. I keep my pace slow as I continue moving. I don't dare peek in for fear of being seen.

"I hope I learn fast enough. I don't want to make them angry."

"Oh hush dear, learning to cook is an art and takes time. And the Lords of the castle won't even notice. Everything will work out perfectly." Her voice fades as I move farther down the hall.

I concentrate ahead on a section that's still well-lit and look at the paintings on the wall. They're massive and the colors are slightly faded as if they've been up for centuries. They must be of family. The brothers all look so much alike and so do all the men in the paintings. Most are of people, of shifters, but some are landscapes. One catches my eye as I get closer to it. There are three swirls, one green, one blue and the largest red. It looks as though it's been painted with fingers. The swirls blend together and are dusted with small ovals, like fingerprints almost. My eyes widen as I realize that's exactly what they are. I squint and look back at the beautiful works of art.

They're intricate and stunning. And then this piece. Is it a child's finger painting?

"It was our mother's favorite." A deep voice startles me and makes me jump back as I turn around, put my hand over my heart, and stare wide-eyed at Drago. The pounding in my heart returns with a vengeance. My mouth parts in shock and no words dare to leave me. The man's eyes flicker, and he tilts his head while asking, "Did Drago give you permission to wander?"

Fear grips every inch of me and chills travel down my arm. I swallow and think about lying to him. But I'm a shit liar. His brow cocks as he waits for my answer and all I can do is I shake my head no.

He chuckles and says, "I didn't think so." He looks down the hall and lets out a sigh that's far too casual. "Do you really think it's wise to upset your Master?" His brow raises in question and anger seeps into the heart of who I am. No one is my master. I would rather die. I take a hesitant step toward him and gather my courage to tell him exactly that. I raise a finger, although as soon as I do, I instantly regret the move. Drago's brother, I'm guessing Galen, stands tall with his shoulders squared, daring me to speak with disrespect. I consider biting my tongue, but then I'm not given the choice.

The shifter takes in a heavy breath and his eyes flash reptilian and blue, his beast. It startles me and I instantly take a step back. He steps forward with a hastened need as something changes in his expression that I cannot place, and he presses his body against me taking a heavy inhale of my neck. I stare up with fear as he grabs my wrists and pins them above my head with one hand. He looks crazed as his breath comes in ragged intakes. "Your smell." He says the words like a prayer. Fear collapses my lungs. My chest hurts and my legs go out from under me. I've never felt so vulnerable in my life. The need to fight is dimmed, but a different kind of agony grows. Regret for leaving the safety of Drago's bedroom.

Before I can process anything, his eyes widen, as if realizing what he's done and knowing how scared I am. I'm barely able to notice it but before he has a chance to back away and apologize, a loud snarl echoes down the hall. I turn to my right, down the way I came, and red eyes are the only thing I can see from the darkness. I can barely swallow, let alone move. Fear paralyzes me.

Slowly the form of a dragon comes into view. Low piles of smoke breathe from his snout. Scales shine and seem to glow in the low light from the flickering torches. Heavy steps shake the floor as he approaches, stalking toward us.

Drago. Something inside me knows it's him.

His brother releases his grip on me, looking between the two of us. I close my eyes and feel caught between the two of them. When I open them, his brother is gone and Drago stands before me naked. Drago's eyes look past me, on the shadow of his brother blending into the darkness. Drago's shoulders rise and fall, his fists clench so tightly, his knuckles are white. Fury radiates off him.

An intense weight, heavy and painful, presses against my heart.

"Drago?" I whisper but he doesn't move. He doesn't look at me.

I take a step toward him and reach out a hand to him. "Drago?" He doesn't respond. He only continues to stare into the darkness. I drop my hand and look down the hallway to see nothing. When I look back at him, his eyes are on me. His gaze intense and the low light from the fire emphasizes the hard lines of his jaw and high cheek bones. His eyes blaze red.

I gasp and take a step back, but my back meets the hard castle wall.

He huffs through his nose and a bit of smoke is revealed. He unclenches and clenches his fists, as if debating what to do. All the while my heart pounds uselessly.

His gaze cuts into me and then his expression hardens even further, his eyes darken like the stormy sky. "Get back in bed." He commands me with a force that has my knees buckling. My heart aches with the disappointment in his tone.

My legs grow weak as I turn and scramble to get to his bedchambers. Never in my life has someone given me what Drago has. His kind touch and generosity. He didn't have to help me. He didn't have to do any of this. As I race toward the bedroom door, I can't hear him behind me. Alone and shaken and filled with regret, I seek sanctuary in his bed and pray it will be enough to save me.

CHAPTER 9

THE MOMENT I SWING OPEN THE DOOR, MY grip so strong I could break the knob, I'm filled with an anger and possessiveness I've never known. She says the one word I never want to hear on her lips.

"Red." The single word trembles, and when I glance at her small form braced with the comforter clinging to her, she manages to say it again but her voice cracks. "Please red. Red."

The raging fire inside is dimmed by the genuine fear in her voice. She scoots back ever so slightly, her small frame trembling. "Red," she whispers and the rage shatters.

I've never done well with the feeling of betrayal and with that word hurled at me, I shut the door behind me with grave cautiousness.

The resounding thud intensifies the tension in the room.

I glance at her huddled on the bed, clutching the comforter before turning to the window and swallow.

"Red?" I ask her with my tone low yet even, and then dare to look at her once again. She nods her head and tears well in her eyes.

"All right Kara." I respond only so she knows I heard her. It takes everything in me to restrain the emotions roaring inside of me. The only truth that keeps me tamed is that she's fucking terrified right now.

Of me…

She's afraid I'm going to hurt her, and I struggle with how to handle the situation. My knuckles turn white as I ball my fists and walk past the bed to the bathroom. I choose not to look back at her, even though I'm all too aware she hasn't stopped watching me. I turn the water on and let it run ice cold. The white noise of the shower spraying down aids to calm me ever so slightly, but the fire in my chest is blazing and my dragon is pissed. He wants out. He wants *control*. Not only of me, but also of our treasure.

I clench and grind my teeth as the freezing water runs down my body. The chill is barely effective, but I focus on it, on reining in the rage that blazes inside of me. As it hits my chest, a low steam forms in front of my eyes. I need to calm the fuck down. I concentrate on my breathing, keeping my eyes closed. And then I remember that I didn't lock the door. My dragon claws up my throat, needing to get to her. I swear to God if she bolted, I'm not going to be able to contain myself. Without second thought, my body moves, slamming the handle down and storming from the bathroom with un-contained determination.

The water droplets fall from me as I hover over the bed, landing onto the comforter and soaking the floor beneath my feet.

Her gasps and wide eyes are what I'm met with as steam billows from me, evaporating the water. With a glance to my left, the red vision dims and the sudden panic wanes; the door is shut, and the key is right where she left it when she left me. I stare at it for a moment, willing the anger in my eyes to leave. I wouldn't be this fucking worked up if it hadn't been for my brother. The image of him pushing his body against her flashes in my eyes, and I bite back the flame that ignites in my chest. I roll my shoulders and relax my stance. I have her now. I have my little treasure.

After clearing my throat, I stalk to the door and I quickly lock it. With my back to her, I allow a moment to pass, listening to the adrenaline rushing in my ears and preparing to fix this little mess. *We'll get past this.* I almost whisper it out loud.

"Did he hurt you?" I speak with my back to her, still facing the door with my eyes closed. I can't face her; I can't risk her seeing my anger.

"No." Her answer is softly spoken. I breathe out and wait a moment to continue. She's all right. She's safe. And he didn't threaten to challenge my claim. My eyes open as I come into clarity. Both of my brothers scented her. And neither has questioned my possession of her. My dragon calms at the realization. There is no threat to my treasure. *She's mine.*

An odd sensation comes over me, a desperate need to claim her and finalize my possession of her. *My mate,* my dragon paces in agreement. *Mine to have. All mine.* I'm only vaguely aware of how the thoughts entered my mind. My dragon is desperate. The parts of me that crave to be fated to her overwhelm my logic and reason.

The intrusive thoughts are cut off at the sound of her hushed cry. A faint feminine sound that brings me to my knees. I can fix this. I can make things right again. I am a worthy mate. She will love me, and she will love what I do to her even more. With a plan in mind I slowly turn to see my Kara and a thud drops in my chest.

The long sleeves have fallen down her arms, no longer neatly rolled like they were earlier today. Her hair is ruffled, and her eyes are wide with both sorrow and fear. Her cheeks are tear stained. I want nothing more than to comfort her, than to take her cheek in my hand and to kiss her tenderly. Her chest rises and falls as she stares back at me. Intent on doing what I must, I step forward but then I remember…red. She's denied me. She safeworded me. Carefully and slowly, I stop at the end of the bed.

"Why did you use your safe word?" I have to ask her even though I already know why.

"Because you're angry with me." Her voice is shaky and breaks on the end.

"Of course I am. Is it because you don't want to be

punished?" That's the reality of the situation. She took her reward; she should be ready to take her punishment. Heat travels down the length of my arms to the palms of my hands, itching to touch her. To teach her what happens when she leaves me.

"No. Please don't." I hate the dreadfulness of her tone.

"Why's that?" I ask.

"I'm sorry I disappointed you."

I shake my head and respond, "You disobeyed me. You deserve to be punished Kara." I make sure to use Kara and not the pet name I love to use for her. With cautious movements, I lay on the bed, but keep my distance from her.

My dragon and I both crave to hold her and comfort her fears, but she's denying me. *She's denied us.* The voice hisses in the back of my mind.

"Please don't hurt me." The sadness in her voice overwhelms me and causes my dragon physical pain. She has no idea what she does to us. How much control she already has, and I barely know her. Turning to look at her, I wait a moment before slowly reaching out, making my movements known. She watches with her lips parted and bated breath.

I take her small hand in mine and kiss her palm. The simple touch soothes the beast inside of me. The scent of her, the feel of her warmth…it's calming in a way I've never known.

Rubbing a soothing circle on her wrist, I confide in

her. "I will never hurt you, Kara." Her eyes, glassy with tears, meet mine. "I promise you. I do not get enjoyment from causing pain. I will never do that to you."

I will her to believe me, but she has no idea what to expect. She is reckless, she is young, and she is human. The logical side of me is reminded that it's very possible she cannot mate. A human and a dragon…it's unheard of and yet, I feel this way. Perhaps I am losing my mind.

Doubt creeps in further and I give her a tight smile as her shoulders curl and she shrinks away from me. I'll give her one out. I have to. I can't keep her here if she truly doesn't want this. Deep inside I know she does, but if she can't admit that to herself, then I'll have to let her go.

"If you want to leave. Do it now." She stares back at me in shock. "I'll have the servants get you everything you'll need." I look deep into her eyes as I speak the next words. "I want you to stay. I want you here with me, but if that's not what you want, then you can leave now." It fucking kills me to say the words, the pain is brutal. My dragon leaps and claws in my chest, refusing to allow her to go. But I endure it, I have to. I have to give her the opportunity to leave. I just pray she doesn't.

After a moment of silence, she shakes her head, her breathing calming ever so slightly. I need more than that.

"Do you want to leave?" Even as I say the words, I don't know that I would hold myself to them. It feels fair and just to offer, but lies are spilling from my lips…as if I could ever truly let her go. "I'll give you everything you'll need to start fresh, Kara." It would be maddening.

She murmurs a response that eases the burden for me. "I don't want to leave."

Rolling onto my side, I face her and ask, "Do you want to stay with me, at least for a little while?" I run my thumb over her cheek, and she leans into my touch.

"Yes." I enjoy the feel of her for a little longer, listening to the steady cadence of her pattering heart calming. With a sad smile at my lips, I know she's not going to like this next part, but we need to get past it.

"Treasure, I need to punish you. And then you won't be so afraid."

She stills beside me, her wide fearful eyes beg me and all I want to do is ease her worry. And I will.

"You want to stay; you will learn to take everything I give you."

Her heart hammers and her breath quickens as the seconds pass, but she doesn't try to leave me. "How?" she finally asks.

Relief is a blessing and a curse. Desire and need rage through me as I command her, "Lie on your back and spread your legs." She gasps and inches away from me, banging her back onto the headboard. "Treasure"—my voice is laced with a threat—"do as I say." I'm not going to fuck her. I debate on telling her that, but I don't fucking want to. I want her to listen to me. I want her to obey me. My voice is stern as I add, "Now." I stare into her eyes as she slowly lies on the bed. She shudders and closes her eyes. It doesn't escape my knowledge that I am still very much naked, very much hard for her.

My blood burns in my veins as I sit beside her, ignoring the pacing of my dragon. I run a calming hand down her arm and the touch is everything I didn't know I needed. I push her sleeve up and take her hand in mine. "Good girl." I kiss the racing pulse on her wrist. Her eyes are still closed. I rub soothing circles over her wrist and speak slowly. "I'm not going to hurt you, treasure." Her breasts rise as she takes a deep breath. "Do you believe me?"

After a moment of silence, she answers, "Yes."

"I don't want you to lie to me. I haven't done anything that I know of that would make you think that I'm a liar." I pause to let the first part really sink in for her. I kiss her wrist again and place a gentle hand on her hip. "But I also know that trust is earned." Her eyes open and find mine. They widen with surprise and her hazel gaze holds so many questions. Her curiosity is my ally.

"I'm disappointed that you left me, treasure. That you were reckless, and you have unknowingly caused problems for me that cannot be undone." I swallow, thinking of my brothers for only a moment before deciding they will be dealt with after, and only after, I've claimed Kara. "I am only angry because you put yourself in danger. Galen would never hurt you, but my dragon isn't comfortable with you being around other men right now." I almost tell her about her heat. I almost tell her how I wanted to kill Galen for even thinking about fucking her. But I keep my mouth shut. She doesn't need to know why. "And dragons aren't reasonable."

"I didn't mean to." She finally speaks.

"You didn't mean to what?" I question her.

"To see your brother." Just hearing those words makes my dragon rage inside of me. I maintain a calm demeanor on the outside though, tempering my tone.

"I know you didn't, little treasure." I speak calmly. "You only meant to leave me."

Her bottom lip wobbles and she turns her head to the side so she doesn't have to look at me. "I'm sorry." Her words are whimpered.

"What did I do that made you want to leave me?"

"Nothing." I hate the answer she gives me. *Nothing*.

"Something happened, treasure. Tell me why you left or I'm going to have to punish you."

"I don't know. I'm sorry," she whispers into the mattress.

I sigh heavily and put my hand on her thigh. "Spread your legs for me." Her breath hitches and she finally looks at me. Fear blazes in her eyes. I lean down and gently kiss her lips, although hers don't part for me or mold to mine. "I won't hurt you." I kiss her again and close my eyes, once again the touch is one-sided. "And you know what to say to make this stop," I whisper into the warm air between us and take her plump lips with mine again. This time I can feel her relax beneath me; her lips press against mine ever so softly. My words comfort her. I pull back, but she takes my head in her hands and pulls me onto her lips again. I kiss her once more, but then pull away and give her a sad smile.

"Just tell me treasure, why did you want to leave me?"

"I don't know, Drago." Her eyes plead with me to accept her answer, but I refuse. She needs to admit the truth. She needs to say it out loud so she can accept the truth. My heart swells with compassion. My poor little treasure. I will heal every piece of her.

As I move on the bed to position myself between her legs, she opens them farther. "Good girl." I push my hands against her inner thighs exposing her to me. Her pussy glistens with arousal and my cock hardens even more for her. "What word will make this all stop?" A bead of precum forms at the slit of my cock and I do everything in me to ignore the desire and burning ache to slam myself inside of her.

"Red." She answers immediately. I nod my head, keeping my eyes on the opening to her heat. Fuck, I want to take her right now.

I'm not going to lie to myself; I'm going to enjoy punishing her. My dick hardens to fucking steel as I take in her beauty. Her breasts that beg me to cup and knead them. Her rose-pink nipples that harden as my gaze travels down them. Licking my lips, I restrain the depraved thoughts that slip into my mind.

I hope she fucking accepts the truth before I lose my composure. She's a stubborn woman; I don't know how much she's going to be able to take before she cracks, but I know she'll hate me every step of the way until she finally gives me the truth. I lean down and take a lick of her. My tongue dips into her opening and then travels up to her clit. It takes everything not to groan into her warmth and fully divulge into the decadency that is her cunt. I flick her clit with my tongue and keep her hips pressed down as she bucks under the movement before I pull away.

With her taste still on my tongue, I ask her. "Why did you leave me treasure?"

"I don't know." Her words are breathy. She may be enjoying this right now, but she won't be in a minute. I moan into her heat as my tongue dives between her folds. She's so damn sweet. I suckle her clit and just as her back bows, I let go and look down at her.

"You do know, treasure; tell me." She shakes her head with her eyes on me.

"I'm sorry. I didn't mean to." I look back at her with sad eyes before leaning back down to lick and nibble her needy clit. My fingers trace along her folds before I slowly press a finger at her entrance. I keep eye contact with her as I push into her heat. Waiting to hear that fucking word that will stop me, but she doesn't say it. She's so fucking tight, I can already imagine how she'll feel around my cock.

I curve my finger and rub the bundle of nerves that's bound to set her off. Her eyes go half lidded and her breathing turns to pants. Gorgeous—her flushed skin and her expression with little bouts of pleasure are utterly gorgeous. Her body rocks into my hand. I let her fuck herself on my finger. *That's my good girl.* Up until her breathing hitches and her pussy starts to spasm. I quickly pull my hand from her and push her hips onto the bed to keep her still and pinned. Her eyes pop open and she gives me a look that could kill. And that's the moment it hits her. I can't help the smirk that lifts my lips up as I stare down at her. Both of our hearts race.

"Sorry, treasure. Not until you answer me."

"I told you, I don't know," she answers this time with spite. I smile at her anger. It reminds me of her strength. My beautiful little treasure can handle this.

She grips the sheets beneath us as I wait a moment and then continue my ministrations.

I run my two fingers teasingly on the outside of her clit and then pinch it lightly. She moans and writhes beneath me. I love that I'm giving her pleasure, but I hate that I won't be letting her come. No one enjoys being denied. I dip my fingers back into her heat and curve them up, massaging her g-spot. Her chest reddens and her cheeks flush a beautiful hue. My little treasure thinks she's being smart, trying to hide the fact that she's going to come. But as soon as I see her fingers trembling, I take my hand away. She shoots daggers at me.

"I'm not lying!" Her voice cracks.

"Tell me why you left, treasure."

"I don't know! I was stupid; I'm sorry!" I press my lips into a firm line at her self-deprecation. For now, I ignore it, but I make a mental note of her behavior.

I push two fingers into her heat and repress my groan as the tips of my fingers hit a thin wall. *Her hymen.* Fuck, my Kara is untouched. I keep my mouth shut and close my eyes as my dick begs me to fuck her. I close my eyes and continue punishing her tight little pussy.

"Tell me why, treasure. Why did you want to leave?" Her deep moan fills the room and as her back arches, I remove my fingers and leave her craving her release. Her pussy clenches around nothing and tears prick her eyes.

"Why are you doing this to me?" My heart breaks at her strangled words. As if this is torture. Torture is watching your only potential mate leave you in the depths of the night. And she will never know that pain.

"You need to tell me treasure."

"I don't know!" I dip my fingers back in and press my thumb against her clit. She's so close. So fucking close that I hardly touch her before her body starts trembling.

I pull away and a sob racks through her. Her orgasm denied once again.

"Please Drago." Her words sound broken and desperate.

"Just tell me why."

She shakes her head and wipes her tears from her cheeks. I lean down and suckle her clit while my fingers work her heat. Her pussy starts to spasm almost immediately. Like the prick I am, I deny my little treasure again.

I give her a moment to settle, but not so long that the waves of desperation have stopped making her body tremble with need. "Why did you leave me?" I ask as I push my fingers in and massage ruthlessly against her front wall. "Tell me why you wanted to leave." I stare into her beautiful hazel eyes as her pussy clamps down on my fingers.

"Because I'm afraid to love you!" she screams at me and then takes ragged breaths as a look of pain flashes in her eyes.

Her words shock me and still my dragon, even though I suspected all along. To hear the words come from her lips, it makes all the difference. I knew she felt something. But *love*? A fire burns low in my gut and tingles down my spine. I nearly lose control of the beast as he roars forward. The need to claim her is far too strong.

Her breathing is staggered and her wide eyes full of vulnerability as she stares up at me, realizing what she's just said. What she's admitted to herself. Whether it's her heat or something more, there's an undeniable pull that's terrifying as much as it is thrilling.

I finally answer her. "Good girl."

I lower my lips to the shell of her ear and whisper, "Now it's time for your reward."

Returning to my position between her legs, I grip her hips tight in my hands and push her back down onto the bed and dive into her heat, feasting on her. Her thighs wrap around my head and she pushes herself onto my tongue. She's desperate to come and I'm going to make sure she does…again and again until she's limp and sated beneath me.

Moaning into her with nothing but pleasure and want, I suckle her clit until her back is bowed and her heels dig into the mattress. Just before she comes, I blow a low flame against the swollen, glistening clit and smack my hand down, putting out the flame and making her body convulse as her orgasm tears through her. As she finds her much needed release, I look up at my beautiful little treasure with the taste of her arousal on my tongue. Her mouth is parted and her back is arched. Her blunt nails dig into the sheets as she screams out her climax.

I can't stand the need to fuck her. I'm all too aware of the need for comfort afterward, the care that she requires as she crashes down from the highest high, but I'm on the edge of doing something I may regret. I push her legs open so they're wide enough for my shoulders to pass and they fall easily, but as I move, she wraps her hands around my arm and stops me. Her hazel eyes are wide and her breathing is labored.

"Please," she barely whispers as she tugs me to brace myself on top of her.

I have no idea what she's asking, but I'm about to lose my mind. All my blood has gone to my dick. "Lie back down, treasure." My words don't come out as smooth as I want them to and I silently curse myself.

"Please, Drago." I stare at her plump lips and imagine taking them with my own.

"Please what?" I ask.

"Please take me."

Time pauses and my vision blurs with her plea. It's a heady feeling to be desired like she does now. I swallow thickly as my dick jumps at her words. I want her so bad it hurts. I shake my head and when I open my eyes, I see doubt and agony creep into her expression.

"You don't want me?" she barely whispers.

"You don't know what you're asking." I try to reason with her. She's been through a lot today. This would be too much. The hour is late, she hasn't rested, and she's been through hell and back. *It would be wrong.* Just as the thought hits me, so does the scent of her heat.

"I do." She nods against my chest. "Please, Drago. I've never felt this way before."

"That's why it needs to wait, my treasure." I'm practically begging her to stop begging me. I can feel my resolve weakening. The need to rut into her and claim her is primal. My eyes roll back into my head as I imagine ripping into her virginity.

"Please," she begs me. I can't take the fact that she's in desperate need. My dragon roars with the need to claim her. He rages inside of me after what happened with Galen. It feels as though everything is pushing me toward her. I gently pet her thigh and try to will the thoughts of fucking her away.

"I know what to say if I don't want it." She takes my hand in both of hers. "Please Drago, haven't I begged enough? I'll be good for you. I promise." My eyes blaze with fire at her words. She's too good for me. Way too good for me.

Her tongue darts between her lips and she whispers her plea, "Please Drago. I need you."

And that's it. I lose all control and flip her onto her knees.

I push the head of my dick against her entrance and groan as I slowly slip into her heat. I could take it slow; I could go easy. But she feels so good, and her pussy is already milking me for more. She's so close to the edge of her release yet again. My dragon roars and fire burns up my throat as I slam deep inside her. I rip through her virginity and still deep inside her. She's so wet, so soft from her own climax, I know it won't hurt her. But still, she cries out a strangled pleasure. Her back arches and it's my name on her lips. My fingers strum her clit until I feel her get accustomed to my size. I nibble her neck, teasing her with hot licks and open-mouthed kisses. She shivers and mewls with ecstasy.

She feels like heaven and hell. The sweet torture of climbing and the desperate need for wanting more.

"You are mine," I whisper into her ear, letting my breath tickle her sensitized neck. I take one more nip of her earlobe and pull back. And then I let myself take her exactly how I've wanted since I laid eyes on her.

I rut into her, pounding into her tight, needy pussy as she spasms around my dick. Her head pushes into the pillow as she screams out her orgasm. I fist the flesh of her hips and continue pounding into her heat as she comes. Her pussy clamps down hard on my dick. Her arousal drips down her thighs and onto me. The wet sound of me ruthlessly fucking her mixed with her cries of pleasure fuel my need to find my own release. My balls tighten and rise as a low tingling sensation threatens to overwhelm me. My toes curl and I breathe out a flame of fire as I slam into her and find my own release. I grip her hips tight and push deeper into her. She screams my name as I pump slow, shallow thrusts into her until every bit of my orgasm has left me. It's only then that I can catch my breath and realize what I've done.

As I loosen my grip on her, I have to catch her small body and gently lay her down. She falls easily to the bed, and I make sure to kiss her on the crook of her neck. It's still slightly colored from the flames earlier. A beautiful pink. And then I pet her back gently as I pull the covers over her body. All the while my heart rages.

I lie next to her, holding her small body close to mine and kiss her neck as she quickly drifts to sleep. Her exhaustion wins out. I continue to hold her though, long enough to admire her beauty and learn the sound of her calm breath. It soothes me.

I move off the bed and see a small spot of pinkish red on the bed. Fear and anxiety overwhelm me for only a moment, remembering she is only human, and I wasn't gentle in the least. And then I remember her virginity. I watch her for a moment, waiting to see if she's in pain. But she only seems to nestle herself deeper under the covers. No signs of pain. In the morning she'll be sore, I'm sure.

The reality of the situation hits me with a force not meant to be denied. I walk quickly and quietly around the room, blowing out the candles and trying my best not to get too pissed at myself for my lack of control. I blow the last flame out and crawl back into bed. I lie next to her, to my treasure, my Kara, and pull her small body to mine.

My mind races with the potential consequences of what I've done.

CHAPTER 10

WITH THE EARLY MORNING LIGHT filtering in the etched glass panes, I wake drowsily and then grin when I feel Kara lying next to me. Her naked body is a glorious sight. Ever so gently, I push her hair off her face and run my thumb along her jaw, careful not to wake her but unable to keep my hands off her.

Her expression is nearly angelic; she is so calm and at peace in her sleep. I clench my jaw remembering last night, the highest of highs and the lowest of lows.

I've never had a woman attempt to leave me before. I've also never wanted to keep one as much as I do Kara.

If ever there was a line, I'm certain I crossed it last night. I wouldn't take it back though, not for a single second. She's mine. In every way, this woman is mine.

That fact doesn't lighten the burden that weighs heavily on my shoulders though. The consequences of what I've done. I sigh heavily and run the hand that's free down my face, stopping at the rough stubble of my jaw. Kara is soundly sleeping on my other arm, with her face buried into my chest. The sheet hardly hides her body from me. The curve of her waist and lush ass tempt me and I'm all too aware of my hardening cock.

Still sleeping, Kara stretches catlike against my body. Her breasts brush against my chest and I stifle a groan. Her leg pushes over mine as she yawns and twists to stretch her limbs. I watch her, waiting for her to realize where she is. I smirk at her as her eyes pop open and she stills against me. Her heart hammers and her eyes widen.

"Good morning treasure." She quickly moves the covers up her body and slowly lies down next to me so that she's barely touching me.

As her gaze looks me up and down, slight fear flashing in her eyes, I remind myself that it's expected. That all of this is new to her. And yet, I fucking hate it. Yesterday morning, she didn't know I existed.

It takes everything in me to maintain my composure. Slowly, she seems to remember every moment, and a warmth colors her cheeks.

A low growl of approval rises in my chest as I readjust under the sheets, my dragon stirring and wanting more. Wanting her naked again. Wanting to spoil her, to have my hands on her.

Although I'm sure she's sore from last night's events, the thought makes my dick stiffen further. I made that pussy sore. I could lick it to make it better.

"Good morning, Sir." She answers, but I don't think she realizes that her use of sir is an indication that she wants to play. I'm certainly up for it, but I have a feeling it wasn't her intention.

"You want to play treasure?" Her eyes fly to mine as I question her.

Her wide eyes, still full of sleep, peer into mine, "Now?"

"You addressed me as Sir," I offer an explanation.

She shakes her head gently, "I don't think so...I, um..." She swallows as she pulls the sheets closer. Rather than allowing her to fumble through thoughts and explanations, I grant her mercy.

"I didn't think you wanted to, either. Calling me Sir is the way to get me to play if you want to, though." She looks at me with uncertainty and clears her throat but doesn't speak.

Her naivety is evident, and she has my sympathy. Which I hope will only aid me in my endeavors. "You can call me Drago."

She smiles but remains quiet. I don't care for her uneasiness, but again I remind myself that it's to be expected. She is human and last night did not go as planned.

"Are you still mad at me?" she asks while holding the sheet to her chest. The insecurity in her voice is worrisome and I loathe it.

"I'm not mad, Kara." With deliberate movements, I grip her chin and tilt her head to look at me and say, "I may have to tie you up before bed though." She clenches her thighs at my words and then lets out a small whimper.

Fuck, that soft feminine noise is everything. I allow a grin to pull at my lips and when her gaze falls to it, she offers me a semblance of a simper. Curiosity and even desire flash in her eyes, although I don't scent her heat in the least.

With my voice low, I contain my own desire long enough to ask, "How are you feeling?"

"Fine," she answers in a whisper and then bites her lip.

"Are you sore?" Her cheeks flush a deep crimson red. It takes a lot of work to keep the smirk off my face. "Part your legs for me."

She looks back at me with wide eyes full of insecurities. "I haven't showered or anything," she says in a hushed tone while tucking her golden locks behind her ear.

The image of her naked body dripping wet comes to mind instantly. We could start the morning with a hot shower, and I could lap the water from her soft skin. It would be far better than the bath. It's an open stall with several shower heads, river rock on the floor, and sleek granite on the walls. It's large and the bench in it would be perfect for her little ass to sit on while I take care of her.

"I know." I stare back at her, waiting for her to obey. "I'd like you not to question my orders." There's a small hint of warning in my voice. She's still getting used to this relationship and power dynamic, so I don't push too much. It's all a part of the play after all.

I fucking love that all of this is new to her. That I have the honor of training and teasing her and breaking her in. My cock twitches once again and on cue, she obeys.

She keeps her eyes on me as she bends her knees and parts her legs. I lean over and brush my fingers along her pussy and open her up for me. Her lips are a bit red and swollen slightly. Hmm. She shivers at my touch and as I slip my fingers up to her clit, she presses herself into my touch.

I take my hand away and rub her thigh intent on rewarding her. "Good girl. I'll take care of you in the shower." She blushes, her legs still spread, and the scent of her arousal tempts me to take her right here once again. Before I can act on it, I command her. "Go now, I don't want to have to wait."

"Oh!" She pops off the bed with a fire lit under her ass and leaves for the shower. With the sheet left behind, her naked body is on display for me and I love it. I crave every inch of her.

Before I join her, I text Sage to make sure she'll have all of Kara's things for her when we get out of the shower. She'll lay them out nicely on the bed and then my little treasure can choose what she'd like. Except for the collar. That is my only must-wear item. I need everyone to know she belongs to me. No one would ever dare hurt her again knowing she's mine.

Whether or not we are mates. Whether or not we will ever be what I crave most is irrelevant. She is mine.

And they will never touch her again. I'll kill them if they do.

I crack my neck as I walk to the door to unlock it for the servants and then make my way to the bathroom. Kara sits perched on the bench in the shower, she's completely dry and just has her hand under the stream. The steam billows around her and the warmth has already made her chest flush with a gorgeous warmth to it. When I get to the opening of the stall, her eyes meet mine and the blush returns to her cheeks. She turns her body slightly, trying to hide her curves. I tisk her as I close the door behind me.

"Never hide yourself from me." I lean down and kiss her lips. At first it's gentle, but then her hand reaches up and she holds my jaw, deepening the kiss. A deep need for more comes over me and I part her lips with my tongue as my hand roams down her side. She sighs into my mouth and leans against me. This is the most affectionate and obedient she's ever been. I wonder if sleepy Kara is more receptive to being a sub than a fully awake Kara. I like both versions, but I really enjoy how easy this is right now. Maybe she just needed a good fuck and a good sleep. Reminding myself what she's been through, I pull away, kiss the crown of her head, and put my hand in the stream. "Is this to your liking, treasure?"

She nods, her lips still parted as she looks up at me. "Yes, Sir."

Fuck, she's being so good right now. I fucking love it.

"Stand up. First I'll wash you and take care of the pain I put you in, and then you'll wash me. Understood."

She smiles again and nods. "Yes, Sir." I put her right where I want her, facing away from me under the stream, and lather my hands up with soap. It's not scented, and I like it that way. I'd rather smell her natural sweetness.

I'll run some oils through her hair to smooth it and give her a touch of floral scent. I gently knead her shoulders and she immediately moans with pleasure. Damn, I love how responsive she's being. I kiss her neck as a reward and she leans back slightly. I should admonish that behavior, but I crave her affection. My dragon presses against my chest, desperate for more.

I'm struck by my own thought. I've never *wanted* anyone's affection before. This little human has gotten under my skin. I smile, move my hands to her breasts, and continue washing her and kneading her body. Mate or not, I think I like how she's got me wrapped around her little finger. So long as she doesn't realize it, so long as she doesn't know the depths I would go to keep her. I gently pluck her nipples between my fingers, and she responds by arching her back and pressing her ass into my now raging hard dick.

"Careful, treasure. I need to heal you first." She shakes her head, pushing her wet hair into my chest.

"I like being sore, Sir." I stifle my groan at her disobedience. My dick pulses nestled in her ass. She smiles broadly, her eyes closed, and pushes her heat against my dick.

"I'll make you good and sore again. I promise you. But I don't want you to be in pain. And above all you will obey me, understood?"

Her feminine simper remains on her face as she nods. "Yes, Sir."

I squat, ignoring my aching needs, to continue washing every inch of her body. It's difficult not to notice that she's still a bit thin, but that will take time. I talk while on my knees behind her. "I want to make a few things clear. Last night, fucking you had nothing to do with your punishment. Nothing at all. You know that don't you?"

"It was a reward?" she questions genuinely. Fuck. No. I don't want her thinking that either.

"No. I fucked you because you were in need." Her eyes fall and disappointment clouds her eyes. I continue my ministrations, more than aware she's upset by whatever I've just said. I clear my throat to continue, and she looks away. "What's wrong?"

I barely hear her murmured question as the water sprays around us. "Is that the only reason?"

Oh. I understand. I rise behind her and run my hands down her sides while I breathe down her neck. She shudders as I whisper in her ear, "No, treasure; I fucked you because I've been dying to be inside you since the moment I saw you." I fucking love the sound of her tortured whimper as she pushes her ass into my dick again. "You better be careful," I warn. "That kind of behavior is going to get you fucked again."

As soon as the words leave my lips, I realize what I

just allowed. She's topping from the bottom. I can't have that happening. Not when she's unaware of everything else at play and what exactly our relationship will entail. My voice comes out harder than I anticipate, "On the bench." She doesn't hesitate. She's so caught up with her desire to please me, my harsh tone doesn't even register. For that I'm grateful. This woman has me stumbling in ways I've never imagined.

I move her how I'd like. I push her knees open, pull her ass to the edge of the bench, and then crouch down to enjoy her how I've wanted to since I woke beside her. With two fingers, I part her lips and slowly lick her from her entrance to her clit. Her hands move to my hair and her head falls back. Her groan is as intoxicating as her taste. As much as I enjoy both, this is about more than pleasure.

Pulling away, I wait for her to look at me. "Keep your hands on the bench treasure." She bites her lip but does as she's told. I return to her reddened pussy and bring the healing heat to my tongue to sooth her ache. I dip my tongue into her heat and savor her taste. So fucking sweet. I lick, suck, and nibble all around her, except her throbbing clit begging for my attention. She moans and writhes, and it's obvious that she's struggling to keep her hands on the bench, but she obeys. Her nails gently scratch at the wood as I tease her. When she peers down at me, desperate for the fall, I praise her for her efforts, "Good girl."

I finally put my tongue flat against her clit and watch

as her body tenses. I know she's on edge and just a little suckling will have her going over. I groan against her heat and massage against her needy clit. I slip one finger in and curl it to tease that sensitive bundle of nerves. I suck her clit into my mouth and massage it with my tongue while my finger goes to work on her g-spot. She goes off under my touch like fucking fireworks. Her legs stiffen and tremble. Her moans fill the shower and sound like a fucking symphony of pleasure. I draw it out of her, sucking and massaging to get it all, every last bit of her orgasm until she's limp and panting.

I pull away from her and find her hands gripping the bench with a death grip. I stand and lean down to kiss her. Her hands wrap around my neck, holding me there for her. I smile against her lips and pull back, grabbing her wrists. "I didn't tell you that you could let go yet, treasure." Her eyes go round with slight worry. That drowsy, lust-filled look is replaced with alertness. I chuckle and kiss her wrists. "Can you stand yet, so you can wash me?"

My dick is so fucking hard, it aches. It stands stiff and tall between us. Begging for attention. I know she's going to want to play. And I can't wait to make her beg for it. *To beg for me.* She smiles and stands, rather firm footed, which is more than I suggested. It's almost like her treat woke her up. I smirk as she reaches for the soap and lets her eyes travel down my body. She gasps when she sees my dick. She bites her lip and doesn't take her eyes away like I thought she would. Her hands find my shoulders, but her eyes are glued to my erection. Her small hands travel my body as she steps closer, bringing her breasts right into my view.

Fuck, she's such a tease. I let her go at her own pace, washing every bit of me as her gaze returns to my cock with each and every stroke she takes. She settles on her knees with her lips just an inch away and rubs her hands over my calves. The water gently hits her back. Her small breasts bounce as she sits on her heels and finally looks up at me as she rinses her hands in the water.

Her hazel eyes flicker with desire as she wraps her hands around the base of my dick and her lips around the head. She closes her eyes and gently sucks. Fuck, her hot mouth is everything I've wanted. One hand on the stone wall braces me, the other reaches for her chin and gently pulls her off my dick. I can't fucking help but to groan as she lets it pop out of her mouth.

"You have to ask permission to pleasure me, treasure." Her mouth falls open in surprise. And her eyes flicker between my dick and my eyes.

"But you're in need." Her response is spoken with complete earnest.

I smile down on my sweet little Kara. "It's my job to take care of your needs, but your only job is to obey me."

"But you're in need." She repeats herself, although she drops her hands and waits for my orders.

"Yes I am. But unlike you I can pleasure myself if I need to." My sweet little treasure narrows her eyes at me.

"It doesn't seem fair that I shouldn't be able to please myself when needed."

"Never said what we're doing is fair. Did I?"

She purses her lips although she's less defiant than anticipated. "No, Sir."

"Do you want to suck me off?" My dick pulses with need at my question.

She presses her lips in a firm line and seems to consider my words. Oh, fuck that. She may have topped from the bottom earlier, but if she's thinking of doing that now there's going to be hell to pay.

Finally, after too fucking long, she relaxes her shoulders and looks up at me and says, with a sweet-as-fucking-can-be voice, "Could I please suck your cock, Sir?"

I don't let my relief show, not the enjoyment I have from this entertaining moment. After all I am in fact in need.

Sliding the rough pad of my thumb over her bottom lip, I answer, "Yes, I want you to take care of me with your mouth."

With a playful glint and a sinful simper, she leans forward and takes me into her mouth again. Her eyes close and her cheeks hollow. I nearly lose it far too quickly when she moans. The vibrations send pleasure through every nerve ending in my body.

Her tongue swirls along the head of my dick and I fucking have to put my hands on the back of her head and push her down father. I need to feel the soft spot in the back of her throat at the head of my dick. She has to stretch her jaw some, but she covers her teeth with her lips and takes almost half of me in. It's more than I thought she'd be able to take. I push my dick down her throat even more and feel her stretch and swallow my length before I pull back.

I find myself bracing against the wall again, the hot shower beating down against my back.

She takes a gasp of air and immediately goes back to bobbing up and down my length, massaging the underside with her tongue.

Before I can stop myself, I find my release. My legs go weak, and I stand paralyzed as a tingle shoots up my spine and my balls tighten. I don't mean to, but watching her enjoy herself sets me off and I don't have time to stop myself. She moans as I release in the back of her throat. I put my hand on her neck to keep her there until every last drop is out of me. As I pull back, I see her swallowing with a look of pride. She's fucking perfect. On her knees in front of me, taking me on like she fucking owns me.

Slightly out of breath, I smile down at her and offer her my hand. She accepts it with a small smile until her eyes look down at my still-hard dick. Her mouth drops in shock, and I chuckle at her. Yeah, once isn't going to be enough with her. I don't think I'll ever get enough.

"Do you want me—"

I shake my head and cut her off. "No."

Her eyes fall as she asks, "Did I not do it right?" It takes me a moment to realize her question is meant to be taken seriously. I came in under five minutes and she's questioning if she did it right?

"Yes, my treasure." I kiss her neck and then her lips.

She molds her lips to mine and leans into me. I pull back and wrap an arm around her to lead her out of the shower and over to the vanity. "You were perfect, in fact." It may be hypocritical of me, but the idea that she was that fucking perfect because she's practiced before hits me and I can't contain the jealousy that creeps in. I keep my voice calm as I ask, "Have you done that before?" I know she was a virgin, but I'm not sure quite how inexperienced she is.

She shakes her head and swallows thickly before answering, "No. I've never done anything like this." It's unexpected how much that pleases me. To have her in ways no one else has.

I wrap a towel around her and have her sit at the vanity. The door opens with a creak and takes my attention back to the events of the day and I make a note to be quick. If that's her breakfast, I don't want it to get cold. I grab a mix of oils from the cabinet and rub them in my hands before slowly raking my hands through her hair. It will leave her hair shiny and smooth. Her pale skin is perfect. Her neck is tall and slender. Her eyes are worn and slightly darkened underneath, but with healthy eating habits and plenty of sleep and relaxation, that will fix itself. Kara is most definitely beautiful. How no one else has claimed her I'll never understand. As our eyes meet in the mirror, I tell her sincerely, "You are beautiful." I rest my hand at her throat and grasp her chin with my thumb and finger to tilt her lips to mine.

When I pull back, her eyes are still closed and she

swallows thickly. "Drago?" Her tone makes me worry. I search her face, but I don't know what to expect.

"Yes, Kara?"

She finally opens her eyes and asks, "What are you going to do with me?" Her voice is calm and even as though there's only curiosity in the question, but her eyes are burdened.

Of all the things to ask, it's *that* question? My heart aches for her. I know what she wants to hear. I remember what she admitted last night, about her fear of falling in love with me. And yet, I've kept her, I've fucked her. And I expect her to stay without giving her the security I know she desires. I want her. I want her more than I've wanted anything. Almost anything. I want a family. I want dragonlings. The truth is, her heat has waned. If she isn't scenting of pregnancy in the next day or so, then there is little hope of her being a mate for me. My heart clenches in pain at the thought as I stare back into her eyes.

"I told you I'm keeping you."

"For how long?" she questions, and I stare back not knowing how to answer. Somewhere deep inside me a primitive need for her begs the answer *forever.* "You said you wanted to heal me, but you already have."

I answer honestly. "I intend to always take care of you. Whether that means this or something else." As I say the words and watch her face fall with disappointment, my stomach drops. I fucking hate myself. She's given me all of herself and I can't promise the same in return. I lift her chin up to give her a kiss, but she pulls her head to the left and out of my grasp.

"Kara." I nearly growl. She turns to face me with a look that could kill and tears in her eyes. I almost lose my resolve. "I will not make promises to you before I know whether or not I can keep them." That voice inside me whispers, *yes you can*. I shake the thought away and look back to my Kara. "I'll take care of you. Every bit of you. Physically and emotionally. Let that be enough for now." Although I haven't worded it as a question, I know my eyes are pleading with her.

"Just one more question?" she asks hesitantly.

"What is it?"

"Am I just a pet to you?"

"No, Kara. You mean more to me than that," I answer immediately and cup her chin in my hand to stare into her eyes as I answer. I want her to *feel* my sincerity. I want her to know that what I say is the truth.

She swallows and nods her head but looks back to the mirror with her shoulders squared and her spine straight. I can practically see her putting on her armor as she leaves me for the safety of the bed. I'm all too aware that her response is well deserved.

CHAPTER 11

IT FEELS AS IF I'VE LOST WHO I AM.

I know better than to rely on anyone or to even expect them to stay around. All of my life I've known that no one is forever. But ever since Drago's taken me, I'm at war with that very truth. I find myself relaxing, feeling as though I no longer need to fight, yet at the same time, I'm waiting for the other foot to drop. I already know what's to come though, no matter how much I wish it weren't true.

This is nothing more than a game to him. He's said as much himself. I'm a pet. And maybe he'll offer me enough money to survive on my own and safety as a reward when he's done with me. Enough to be taken care of. But either way, he will be done with me at some point and then what will I be left with? This bleeding heart of mine that should have known better.

It takes a moment for my heart to feel full again. I feel pathetic. I practically told him I loved him yesterday. I gave myself to him. As a faint rainfall taps at the glass pane windows, I turn my attention to it and remember last night. Pulling the covers in close, I know all too well I'd do it again. I don't regret it in the least. Running my fingers through my hair and inhaling the sweet floral scents of the oils, I know the same is true for this morning. I've never felt so full and so complete. I loved everything that happened last night in this bed.

That's the fault of it all though, isn't it? I'm falling hard for him because no one has ever touched me like that. No one has ever wanted me and I've damn sure never wanted another soul. There's a faint sound beyond the closed bathroom door and my heart pauses, waiting for the door to open. Yet it doesn't. It's quiet yet again as I sit alone on his bed.

Once again that feeling overwhelms me. The one that scolds me for being so pathetic. I want to bow at his feet. Fuck, if he told me to kiss his feet I would. I'd do anything he told me to. But I don't know why.

How does he have me wrapped around his little finger like that? I've never been this way. I've never opened myself up like this. I never wanted to, either. But he forced it out of me. Logically, I know he treats me better than anyone else ever has. He gives me more than I ever thought I would have. How could I not fall for him when he cares for me as he does?

Not to mention he's handsome, powerful, and radiates a sex appeal like I have never known. He's practically a god among mortals. More so than any supernatural I've ever met. Even compared to his brothers, the air seems to bend around him. That doesn't make keeping my guard up easy. The bathroom door opens, and he beckons me with a simple "come."

My body instantly obeys and that warmth flows deep within my belly.

Pet. Nothing but a pet, my inner voice hisses, and yet it does nothing to slow my pace to meet him in front of the sink. "Turn," he commands me, adding a twirl of his finger, and I do as he says. I stare back at him in the mirror. Both of us completely bared to one another, but only one of us holding any power at all. It's quiet and I search his expression for any hint at all as to what he has planned for me, but he gives nothing away. As if reading my mind he informs me, "I want to pamper you and make sure you're presentable."

He brushes my hair and barely touches me as he does. "Nearly done," he tells me, and I already miss him caring for me like this.

All the while, my heart patters wildly and I close my eyes to focus on calming it. He must know what he does to me. I imagine he enjoys it.

He tells me to go relax on the bed while he readies himself and I do.

He tells me to come to him and I do.

If he told me to get on my knees right now, I would. What is wrong with me?

I open my eyes and stare into his heated gaze. I know he's still hard and I want nothing more than to feel him inside me once again. I crave that ache between my thighs to come back with a vengeance. But I already begged for his touch once. I promise myself I'll hold out this time. I clench my thighs as he pulls me closer to him, motions, and walks me back into the bedchambers.

His hand grips my hip, skin against skin, and his touch is fire to my blood. My breathing is ragged, my head is cloudy with lust, and my thoughts run wild with what he'll do to me next time I'm vulnerable beneath him.

He stops me just shy of the bed, him to my back, and I stare at the clothes with disbelief. Tears prick at my eyes as I stare at the most luxurious clothes I've ever seen. "For you, my treasure," he murmurs in my ear and his warm breath tickles down my shoulder. When he releases me, I walk hesitantly closer and trail my fingers along the silk negligees and chiffon dresses. My bottom lip drops and I don't have the ability to close my mouth. They're gorgeous. With that thought, I stare back at him as if it's a cruel joke.

"All for you," he tells me with a look of sincerity, and I can barely swallow. I pick up a few cotton blouses and hold them against me. I've never had nice clothes. I look at the jewelry in black velvet boxes sitting to the right.

With emotions overwhelming me, I question, "Why are you doing this?" I just don't understand. For a split second a semblance of who I am returns and I'm terrified of all of this. I would rather it be over so I can pick myself up off the floor once he's done with me.

"I don't want these." My voice cracks and I fucking hate that it betrays the façade I'm aiming for.

His thick brow knits and his eyes narrow slightly, as if confused or disappointed, I'm not sure which. His tone though is logical and one of reason. "You have nothing to wear. You will wear them."

"I do not want to be bought and paid for with pretty things I do not need."

He looks at me bewildered before closing the distance between us, taking my hand in his, and kissing the back of it. It calms both of us. He takes a deep breath and speaks evenly to me. "You need clothing. Whether you like that or not. I simply bought you what I like. If there's nothing here that you like, we'll take it back and get you something else."

I search his eyes for something that makes this seem okay. But I find nothing. A hard lump grows in my throat. I turn to look at what he's bought me. These expensive clothes make me feel cheap. I wish I could just be happy and enjoy this, but now I'm second guessing everything. If only he'd give me a straight answer. None of this feels right and that nagging feeling that all I'm doing is setting myself up to be hurt returns full force.

"Kara?" My name on his lips sounds more like a plea and I face him, feeling raw and torn. His eyes darken with a deep primitive need as he takes one more step closer to me. My Dom. The shifter I'm afraid to love. The dragon I know is going to burn me.

"Yes?" I dare to whisper.

"I want you to wear these. I want you to look beautiful for me. Will you wear them to make me happy?" he asks carefully, staring deep into my gaze. That power he has over me floods my very being. I feel myself giving in; after all, I haven't much of a choice. Not when I can so easily compare what he's capable of to what a mere human like myself can do.

"I'll wear them for you, Sir," I answer.

"Good girl." He reaches across me to pick up something off the bed. "Especially this." He lifts my hair off my shoulders, and his heated touch sends a shiver of want through me. With my eyes closed, I allow him to do whatever he'd like. I hear a click and look down, but I can't see anything. I can feel a weight on my neck, but I'm not sure what it is. It's obviously a necklace…or collar as he called it. As he rounds to stand in front of me, my eyes open and I find him staring at the collar with a wicked twinkle in his eyes. My fingers itch to touch it, so I do. It's a heart, a little larger than the size of my thumb and on a surprisingly thin chain. "It's perfect."

"What does it say?" I ask as I feel the engraving but I'm unable to read it since it sits at the dip in my collar.

"That you're mine." The way his hard, sensual voice says those words makes me clench my thighs yet again. If nothing else, what happens between us will leave me ruined for all other men. He already has me. He's already won. Any fight would be a losing battle.

Not waiting for a response from me, Drago examines a large silver tray that was brought in earlier.

The colorful array of fresh fruits is paired with cured meats and cheeses. There's enough food on the large tray for a small village. On cue, my empty stomach growls and I'm surprised how hungry I am given I just ate last night.

I near the tray as Drago busies himself with arranging some of the food onto a small dish. There are dozens of eggs all still in their shell on a plate under a glass dome. Two silver cups and bone spoons sit next to the eggs. I assume that means the eggs have been boiled. Next to that is a heaping pile of meat slices. My eyes travel behind the meat and eggs to a melon that's been cut in half and each half filled with berries.

"Seven-minute eggs. I think you'll enjoy them." He quickly clears the clothes from the end of the bed and puts them in a pile on top of the dresser. "I'll have them put them away for you."

I shake my head and furrow my brows. "No." His dark eyes reach mine slowly. My breath hitches. Is this the first time I've told him no? I breathe in deep and stand my ground. I enjoy being his pet. I love how he commands me. But I don't want someone doing these things for me. Sneaking in and out of the room to provide for me in ways I'm capable. I square my shoulders and prepare to defend myself, but before I get a word out, he speaks.

"All right," he states easily enough, bringing the tray to the bed and not seeming to notice the battle warring inside of me at all. He adds without sparing me a glance, "Let me know if there's anything you don't want." Then he motions for me to sit at the top of the bed by the pillows. It's only then that I realize someone has already made the bed. It makes me feel uneasy. "I'll have Sage come as well and show you the shops around the village."

A pit settles in my stomach. "I'm not sure I'd like that."

Drago glances at me with what I think is confusion and then begins setting up a plate for me. He can do these things for me. I like that. But others that I don't even know—it just feels wrong.

"Kara," he starts with a firm voice. "There are things you're going to have to get used to. What would make the transition easiest for you?" There's no compromise in his voice and he looks back at me expectantly.

A beat passes and then another of me standing at the end of the bed and him waiting for me to obey. To give in. To do as he says and be his perfect little pet. "I'm not sure anything would make having strangers wait on me any easier. I don't feel—"

"Would you like it if you knew them better so they weren't strangers?" he questions, interrupting me. His patience is infuriating.

My tone is a little harder. "I'd like it if I could just do these things myself."

His tone remains even as he answers, "I will consider it. As far as going into town, you'll be doing that. I need for you to get used to your surroundings. I've been told the best way for a woman to do that is to shop with other women." His words hit me in a weak spot of insecurity. I wonder how many women have done this. My cheeks flame. How many are still in this castle? Drago interrupts my thoughts with a question. "What's got you so upset?"

Everything in me is telling me to hide my insecurity, to leave this issue alone, yet my mouth opens and the words fall out. With my hands trembling, I dare to question, "How many women have you made your pet?" Anxious heat flows through my body as he motions for me to sit once again.

"Come and we can talk about these things over food."

"I'm not sure I'm hungry," I tell him and in that moment my body betrays me. My stomach growls and I'm instantly embarrassed. "Sit," he commands me, and I decide to obey, forcing myself to sit at the head of the bed with him.

He passes the plate to me and tells me to eat. I obey, opting for a tart raspberry as I stare at him and wait for his response. It's delicious. Of course it is. Everything is divine here and none of this is truly meant for me.

Drago inhales deeply as he cuts up the meat on his plate. Finally he offers a response, "I'm much older than you treasure, and I doubt you'd like the answer."

That's an acceptable answer, I suppose. But I continue my questioning, "How many that still live here?"

His brow arches as he pauses his cutting to question me, "Is that what you're worried about?"

"Yes," I answer without taking a single breath. "I want to know."

His voice softens and he leans down to kiss my

cheek. "None. It's been a very long time since I've wanted a woman."

The relief is notable at simply knowing there isn't anyone else. I allow that information to sink in.

My brow furrows with curiosity, "Men?"

He smirks at me. "No. No one, for a very long time."

"So, there's only me."

He nods, adding, "It is only us." His words do something to me I can't describe.

"Tea?" He offers a cup to me I hadn't seen, and I gratefully take it.

"Thank you."

The silence between us is easy as we both eat. Just like last night, everything is delicious. I watch as he taps the bone spoon against the shell and eats his egg. And then another and another. It'll take him all damn day to eat breakfast the way he is.

"Do you usually have all this for breakfast?" I can't imagine he gets a thing done if he does.

"Usually a mountain of red meat. I like steak. A lot of steak. All day." I have to laugh at his straightforward admission.

"Then why all this?" I gesture to the tray and our plates.

He peers at me with a look in his eyes as if I should know. "I wanted you to have a nice breakfast." I swallow down the sip of hot tea and smile back at him. All of those emotions going back and forth settle down if for no other reason than that I'm grateful.

Just as the fluttering in my chest picks up again and threatens to have me overthinking everything, a knock at the door interrupts us. My eyes widen as I realize I'm not at all decent.

"One minute." Drago calls out with a deep baritone voice. He moves quickly from the bed to the pile of clothes and pulls out a light blush nightie that seems to be made of tiny pieces sewn together like petals of a flower. It's nicer than any dress I've ever worn.

"Wear this," he tells me, handing me the delicate clothing, and I'm taken aback by how soft it is. It's luxurious for a simple night gown. It slips on easily enough, loose yet hugs my curves in a way that's elegant, and stops just above my knees in the front yet longer in the back. I'm so enthralled with the gown, I'm caught off guard when Drago opens the door.

One of his brothers walks in and it takes me a moment to know that it's Galen. I remember that Cyrus has a small scar on his chin. It's uncanny how alike the brothers look. I glance between Galen and Drago and grin at the telltale differences between them. Galen has a slightly sharper chin. Good. I won't confuse them all now. That will put an end to me thinking every dragon is Drago.

"Galen." Drago is short with his brother and seems uneasy with him being here. He opened the door, but he stands in between Galen and me, as though he's protecting me. The smile falls from my face. I hesitantly move to the back of the bed. For some reason it's become my safe spot. An uneasiness creeps through me. I'm reminded of Victor, of talk of war. A sickness threatens to rise up my throat.

Galen puts his hands up, palms out. "I only came to apologize."

"Apology accepted. You can go now." Galen flinches, appearing hurt by Drago's curt response.

Drago shifts his weight and sighs. "My dragon is still on edge."

"I understand. I'd like to apologize to your…"

"Kara," Drago cuts him off.

"To your Kara," Galen finishes, although he's yet to look at me. He speaks only to Drago. "I didn't mean to frighten her or get your dragon riled up. I didn't know she was in heat." He says the last line with a bit of an admonishment, and it takes a moment for me to even register his words. *Heat.* He scents the air deeply and adds, "Besides, her heat is gone now, your dragon should be fine."

I look at them both in confusion and ask, "Heat?" A prickle of nervousness runs through me. Heat is for werewolves. Heat is for breeding. Humans do not do such things.

My heart races as Galen's wide eyes meet mine. I can't meet his gaze so instead I stare at the sheets. Right beneath me, Drago took me last night. My breath comes in shorter pants.

Heat. The realization is slow to come over me and panic sweeps in as the puzzle pieces fall into place.

That's why he fucked me. That's why he's keeping me.

To breed me. It's why he's nice to me. I knew it was too good to be true. Betrayal sweeps over me as my throat closes tightly while Drago and his brother have a heated and hushed discussion.

Tears prick my eyes as I recall so many conversations centered around dragons. I remember them talking about Isabella only days ago. I remember what the sorcerer said about their need for heirs.

Drago only wants young. He just wants to breed me. I look up at Drago with tears in my eyes. That's why he can't tell me how long he wants me to stay. My heart falls into the bottom of my stomach and shatters. I scoot off the bed rather unladylike and ignore Drago as he calls after me. I slam the door to the bathroom with trembling hands and try to lock it, but there's no fucking lock.

Somehow I hear Galen leave after a few shouted words from Drago as I pace the small area in front of the vanity. Drago walks in with an air of dominance, but I look straight back at him without displaying the very real fear I feel. My gut churns and my body chills with a cold sweat.

"You lied to me." The words erupt from my lips with malice. I can hardly hear anything over the sound of my heart trying to beat out of my chest. *Heat.* That's why I'm not myself. It wasn't a spell. It's something unnatural that's taken hold of me. It must be. I'm only human. We don't "heat." As questions pile up, so does the agony of knowing I was being used.

"You don't understand, treasure." I fucking hate that he's using my pet name right now.

"Don't you dare call me that," I scream at him. He blanches at my anger, but I don't give a shit if I've surprised him. If I'm not being a good *pet*. "You didn't just want to fuck me. You wanted to breed me!"

"No, my dragon was attracted to you before I scented you." He puts both his hands up as if in surrender, but as he takes a step toward me, I take a step back. He's far too close, too powerful, too on edge, and my heart won't stop racing. My legs bump into the seat at the vanity with an unfortunate step back. I fall and land hard on my ass and try to brace my myself. I'm not as successful as I'd like. I wince from the pain and grab my wrist. That fucking hurt.

Before I know it, he's on his knees next to me holding my wrist in his hands. His scent engulfs me as does his warm touch and I hate it. I snatch my wrist away.

"Don't fucking touch me." I'm barely able to speak through clenched teeth. "You don't get to touch me anymore."

He takes a sharp inhale and looks deep into my eyes. I don't drop his gaze. I hope he knows how fucked this is. I can't believe I fell for him. My heart sinks deep down and twists into a painful knot. Tears leak down my face, but I don't break eye contact. I won't do it. His hand comes out, I assume to wipe my tears, but I shove him away. "Leave me alone!"

"Treasure." I shoot daggers at him for daring to call me that.

I practically spit the word in his face, "Red." I ignore the hurt in his eyes.

"Kara," he attempts to placate me with a warning tone.

"I'm such a fucking idiot. I should've left when I had the chance." I swallow thickly, resolving myself. "I want to leave."

"You may be pregnant." His simple statement is his answer.

"I didn't ask for this," I say and bite back the tears.

"You begged for it."

"Fuck you!" That fucking prick! How fucking dare he throw that in my face. I wanted him because I fucking loved him! Him! Because I was stupid to think he loved me too. This heat, this spell between us, whatever this is, it has a grip on me I could never fight. I was foolish enough to accept his kindness thinking all he wanted in return was me. I swallow the spiked lump growing in my throat.

"I didn't mean it like that. I'm sorry, Kara." He has the audacity to sound sorrowful as I sit hunched over in his bathroom.

I close my eyes and shake my head, hating how badly it hurts. I can't talk to him. "Leave me alone." I can't even look at him right now.

"I'll know soon if you're pregnant." His voice is hard,

but there's a trace of sadness. "You'll stay till then." Tears free-fall down my face as my body shakes with sadness.

Then I'll leave. My body goes numb, and I listen as his heavy steps lead him away from me.

Only after the door is shut, I bury my face into my hands and cry. My shoulders shake and tremble and then I regain my composure. He slams the bedroom door loud enough for me to know he's gone.

I don't want him to come back and find me like this. And I can't lock the damn door. My eyes widen with realization. I can't lock *this* door. I get to my feet and run to the bedchamber's door. It's already shut so I quickly shove the key in and turn, just the way he did last night.

I lock him out. If he won't let me leave, then he certainly cannot stay. I may not have anything else in this life. But at least I'll have one moment to put distance between us and cry in peace. I crawl into Drago's bed and pull the cover over my head as the reality sinks in. I was nothing more than a pawn to him. Why does it hurt so much though? I have loved and lost before, better people than Drago. Longer relationships than this. Hurting all over and unable to think straight, I let exhaustion and sadness take me to sleep hoping when I wake up, it will all have been a horrible dream.

CHAPTER 12

"YOU'RE A PRICK GALEN," I PRACTICALLY seethe, allowing my anger to penetrate the thick tension between us. My brother rises from his seat at the dining table as I enter the hall. He stands with his hands up in surrender as he narrows his eyes. I want to fucking beat the shit out of him. I want to slam my fist into his face and take out all this anger on him, but there are only rare occasions when violence is needed and now is not one of them. Besides, we made a pact long ago not to fight one another. And it's worked well for us for this long, there's no reason to start a war over a little miscommunication.

Cyrus cocks a brow at me but doesn't move from his seat as I pull mine back, allowing the chair to scrape along the floor, the sound breaking the tension ever so slightly. Even though my dragon paces with worry and my muscles are still tense with irritation, I force myself to sit back. She's angry because I withheld. I know all too well her disappointment is my own doing. She'll forgive me though. I know she will. As I clear my throat, doubt twists my heart in pain, but I push it down. Galen's at the head of the table with me on his right and Cyrus on his left. I put my elbow on the table and flex my hand. I know she'll forgive me. A little white lie is certainly not going to keep her from me.

"You know I didn't mean it, Drago." Galen speaks with sincerity, and I nod in acknowledgment. I believe him. We'd never fuck each other over, but that doesn't change the fact that now my Kara, my treasure, is angry with me.

"She safeworded me because of it." I look Galen in the eyes so he knows how irritated I am.

He smirks at me with a wicked twinkle in his eyes and shrugs. "Not the first time."

A deep crease settles in my forehead as his comment sinks in. I sit forward in my chair with disbelief. "You were listening?"

With a shrug, he replies, "I couldn't help but to be curious." A different kind of possessiveness stirs in me. He better have left before she started moaning my name and coming for me.

"Don't worry, once she agreed to her punishment, I left."

A huff of an acknowledgment leaves me although the irritation stays. "Like I said, you're a prick, Galen." I smirk back and lean deeper into my seat now that my dick is raging hard again. Fuck I need her. I lick my lips remembering her sweet taste from this morning.

"Anyone want to fill me in?" Cyrus questions.

"Drago's pet is dismayed because he failed to mention she was in heat."

Cyrus looks at me like I'm mad, his expression of both shock and disapproval. "Drago. You attempted to breed her without her knowing?"

A pang of guilt hits me, but they fail to understand our needs. "No. It's not like that." I let my arm fall to the table and it lands with a heavy thud. "I intended to wait and see if she went into heat again next month." I frown at my brothers. "I wasn't planning on sleeping with her."

"You have more control than I do brother." Hearing Cyrus's confession has my eyes narrowing in on him. He throws his hands up. "You know I didn't touch her."

"So you have your mate and now I get mine from this deal." Galen says, clapping his hands with a firm grin on his face.

"I don't know that she'll let me bed her again." I run a hand down my face.

"You two have screwed yourselves." Cyrus looks between the two of us. "You take a woman without her knowing, who, sorry to say it Drago, may never heat again. And you," he turns his attention to Galen, "want to kidnap a woman and possibly start a war over someone who *might* be able to carry dragonlings." He shakes his head, his eyes worried. "What the hell is wrong with you two?"

I huff a laugh. "There's more to life than just fucking. Haven't you ever wished for a mate?"

"The idea is intriguing, but you know how this is

going to end, don't you?" He stares at both of us with a grim expression. His pessimistic view is not contagious at this hour.

"When did you become such a depressing asshole, Cyrus?" I ask him from across the table.

"He's been doing that lately." Galen talks only to me as if Cyrus isn't in the room. It makes me grin. We used to do that when we were kids to piss Cyrus off. Years before that, when we were just children, we'd convince him he was invisible because we so often ignored him and talked about him like he wasn't there. I chuckle and keep my eyes on Galen.

"It's unfortunate he has no intention of finding a mate. I imagine it's his lack of confidence in the bed chambers that keeps him to himself."

"Fuck off." Cyrus shrugs and leans back in his seat like he's not affected. Which is a telltale sign that we're getting under his skin.

Galen talks right over Cyrus, "Poor women have no idea. I bet he leaves them all disappointed."

"You two are disgraceful. You know that?" Cyrus speaks but Galen speaks over him.

"Probably best that he doesn't procreate. We inherited the best of the genes after all." He continues, "Wouldn't want our future generations to be little Cyruses running around." I all out laugh at Galen's words, but it comes to an abrupt halt as Cyrus rises onto his feet.

Cyrus yells, "There won't be a next generation! We're fucked. We're all fucked!" He breathes heavily, his face red as his eyes flash reptilian. "Ever since the purge we've been screwed over." He takes a heavy seat and draws his dragon back in. "We're the last dragons; there will be no more."

"What the fuck Cyrus?" Galen voices exactly what I was thinking. My throat is tight with the notion that there is no hope.

"I've tired of this depressing version of you," I add on. We both look at him with a mix of irritation and concern. He's never been like this in his entire life.

He huffs as if he didn't just lose his mind. "Then stop bitching about mates so I can get back to the fun in life."

"We want mates, Cyrus," I stress. "I crave one more than anything."

He looks me dead in the eyes and answers, "Well then you want something you can't have."

"My mate is in my room right now and she will give me dragonlings." My voice holds no conviction; even as I say the words, I doubt them. Cyrus cocks an eyebrow at me as though I've proven his point for him. "She will."

"And when she doesn't?" Cyrus asks as if it's inevitable.

My heart sinks at his question. A beat passes before I tell him, "She's heated stronger than any woman ever has before."

"How many years did we spend trying to find appropriate companions?" Galen and I look at each other with our lips firmly pressed into a flat line. Cyrus continues without either of us answering him. "Too many fucking years. Courting women and waiting to see if their heat would hold." A black air of depression settles between us. "Why not try it my way? Huh? Least I'm having fun with it and there are no broken hearts or grief. Only enjoyment."

"Are you though?" Galen questions him and I'm honestly surprised. "You seem to be more and more passionate about mates recently." He cracks his neck and sighs. "Almost as if you actually want one."

"Of course I fucking want one. But they're all dead. They died with everyone else."

"I refuse to believe it." Galen's quick to answer.

"Same here," I say, strumming my fingers along the table. I can't help but to think of how quickly Kara's heat left her though. Doubt spreads through me more than my dragon cares for.

"I'd be fucking happy for you two to prove me wrong." Cyrus crosses his arms and sits back in his seat. The wooden legs of it creak.

"Well we'll find out soon enough with Drago's pet." Galen smirks at me with confidence, but I want to smack that look off his face.

"Don't call her that," I snap and then shake off my irritation. "She's more to me than a pet."

"Nothing wrong with your mate being your pet," Galen answers with a firm voice and Cyrus nods in agreement.

"I'd rather you simply not call her that."

"Then why tell us that's what she is?" Galen tilts his

head and feigns ignorance. "Oh that's right, so that we stay away and you could have her—and her heat—all to yourself."

I smirk at him and reply, "It worked."

Cyrus smiles broadly in response. "And which one of us is the asshole?"

We all snort a laugh and the tight air between us seems to dissipate. Although some thoughts can never be forgotten and sink their claws into my consciousness.

"So you really think you may have bred her?" Cyrus asks.

"I would hope so."

"Then you'll be stuck with her," my brother states and Galen hints in his question.

"Yes, I'd be content with that." I smile at the thought of her being *stuck* with me. Mated as the stories have told.

"Good to hear since it's been a while since you've been happy with company," Galen says. "She seems as if she can handle you too."

"Yes, she has a little fire in her. You look good together," Cyrus adds.

"Thank you both." It fills me with pride that my brothers approve of her. Not that it's needed, but still it settles some concerns. "She is a little spitfire."

Galen laughs. "Is that your pet name for her? It seems fitting."

I shake my head. "No, it's treasure."

Galen's expression turns serious and his eyes dance with hope. "Also fitting."

"Do you two really think it's possible?" Cyrus looks up at us in a way he hasn't for years. More than anything, he appears wounded and vulnerable. "You think we really could find mates who aren't dragons? These humans could be our mates, real mates?"

"I do, Cyrus," Galen answers and I nod in agreement.

And then I speak words I didn't even know were true until they leave my lips. "Even if she can't bear my children, I still want her. I still want my mate." Fire blazes up my chest and my dragon bats his wings inside of me. He purrs with triumph and agreement. As he presses me for control, the pull to her is strong. I feel a need to go to her. To be with her.

"Even without young?" Galen's surprised, and I have to admit, I'm surprised as well.

I slowly nod my head as if coming to terms with what I've just admitted to myself. "She's more than worthy of being my mate." I look my brother in the eyes. "I would be honored to have her by my side. I want to be loved and it is undeniable that there's something between us that is more than I've ever had."

Galen sits back with a pout on his face. "Is that why you gave me Isabella? You know if you'd still like the chance to court her, I would understand."

Cyrus speaks before I can, "If he wants his pet, let him keep her for fuck's sake."

"Don't call her that, Cyrus," I warn.

"Ooh. Look who's getting all worked up." Cyrus smiles as he teases me.

"That's if she wants you," says Galen. "I didn't mean to cause tensions there, Drago." Galen's reminder that my treasure is angry with me isn't welcomed.

"She'll be all right; she just needs to cool down." They both look at me with doubt and neither speaks a word. "What?" I ask.

"Women are…emotional, Drago." Cyrus mumbles under his breath. "And humans untrusting in general."

"What the hell does that even mean, Cyrus?" He shrugs and Galen holds his stomach while he laughs.

"He means you're in deep shit, Drago," Galen answers.

"She's a good girl. She'll understand. She only needs time."

"All right then, let us know how that goes," Cyrus says as if he knows something I don't.

"I will." I furrow my brows, not liking their confidence that she's going to stay mad at me forever. She can't stay angry that long. "I didn't come here to talk about Kara, let's get on with it."

"Right, right. I'd like to leave as soon as possible to acquire my potential mate."

I cut Galen off. "I don't want to leave her while she's angry."

Galen looks to Cyrus, eager to leave and begin his adventure with or without me. "Do you think just the two of us can handle it?"

"How would I know? I've never been to their estate, have you?"

"No"—Galen purses his lips—"but with so many people on the inside, I'm sure we could sneak in."

Cyrus nods his head. "It's not like many have ever seen us before."

"Eh, I don't want to risk trying to just walk in." He opens his laptop and types in his password. "We could get in through a window. We just need to know where she usually is within the estate."

"In and out as quickly as possible." He turns the computer to face us, and I recognize the same picture as before.

"Is that the only picture you have of her?" I add my concern. "What if she's aged or her appearance has changed?"

Galen purses his lips. "It's the only picture."

"How old is that picture?" I ask.

"A few years." I raise my eyebrows in concern. "I know, but it's the best we can do at the moment. I asked for an image, but my intel has informed me that Alec has become a little possessive of her."

"Possessive? I don't like the sound of that."

Galen clenches his fists. "I know. I don't like it either. That's why I want to leave tonight."

"The more I think about the Authority, the more I don't like any of this," I say, gathering the attention of both my brothers.

"I find it hard to believe that he's truly keeping mates away from us," Cyrus says.

"Mates?" Galen asks.

Cyrus shrugs. "I don't know. Mate…mates? Who knows?"

"Well he has her. So he obviously is." Galen's dragon seems to rise at the thought, and I can see him warring to keep his beast down.

"Is it really intentional though, or is there some other reason?" Cyrus's curiosity surfaces and I smile seeing my brother in his usual state. The distress from the talk of mates seems to have waned.

"What other reason could there be?" Galen asks.

"That's not what I'm talking about brothers." Again, both of them give me their complete attention.

"What do you mean then?" Cyrus questions.

"They don't seem to have control of much. What with towns being prey to supernaturals and wolves fighting each other for territory. What good are they really?"

"They seem to keep the humans and supernaturals separated for the most part."

"Not my Kara. She said she expected to die." Both of my brothers seem saddened and shocked, just as I was. "What is the Authority doing for them? What kind of justice comes from that?"

Galen answers grimly, "They were offered a choice, Drago. If humans don't want protection, that's their choice to make."

"Kara didn't get that choice; she was born into these circumstances." Knowing the injustices she faced makes my dragon push me to check on her, to make sure she's all right.

"I'm sure we could present this issue to the Authority. But at the moment we are planning to steal from them." Galen instantly rages at Cyrus's condemnation.

"We aren't stealing from them!" he yells. "She's rightfully mine!"

"Calm down Galen," I speak calmly. "First off, we don't have fated mates and her abilities are merely speculation." He tilts his head in anger and opens his mouth to argue with me, but I cut him off. "I understand where you're coming from though. They're keeping a potential mate captive to prevent your bonding. I agree that's unlawful of them."

"Don't worry Galen, I'll accompany you." Cyrus stands from his seat and walks over to Galen. "Are you ready brother?"

"Yes." Galen rises as well and puts his hand on Cyrus's shoulder, looking him in the eyes with gratitude. "We'll figure out what to do about the Authority. But first I want my mate."

I nod my head and lean back in the seat, knowing I must go to my mate now. I hope she's over our little spat.

"Good luck with your mate, Drago," Galen says as they leave the room.

Cyrus chuckles before adding, "Yes, you're going to need it."

CHAPTER 13

A RELENTLESS BANGING ON THE DOOR WAKES me from my slumber. I stretch and yawn, feeling absolutely wonderful, and then I remember why I'm in bed. Why my eyes feel slightly swollen. I tighten my grip on the pillow and stare at the locked door that rattles with another loud *rapt, rapt, rapt* knocking.

"Kara, open the damn door!" He sounds furious, and even as my heart races, I swallow down the fear and hold onto my conviction. I'm glad I managed to piss him off. He lied to me, and I don't want him near me.

I almost yell for him to just go away, but then I smile, knowing it'll piss him off even more if I simply ignore him. My smile vanishes as quickly as it came. What I felt was one-sided. His intention was purely to impregnate me. He only wanted to use me and breed me. I clench my thighs and close my eyes in shame. *Why the fuck does that turn me on?*

I shake my head. It doesn't matter that I'm aroused by the notion. This isn't like being his pet, where we both knew every angle of the relationship. This was him *lying* to me. Him using me without me knowing. My heart clenches and the pain shoots through my chest to the point where my palm naturally rubs between my breasts to try to dull the agony.

I still don't understand the pull he has. I don't understand why I feel as I do. But I know he lied to me, and all life has ever taught me is that I should have known better than to trust him.

"Open the door!" He bangs again. "Kara!"

Another hard series of *Bang! Bang! Bang!* jolts my body. I wish he'd just break in or give up; my head is fucking pounding from all the noise.

A moment of quiet passes, and I nearly think he's left, but then I hear his voice, much quieter, but more placating.

"Kara, treasure, please open the door." I can't help but feel a slight shift of warmth inside of me at his gutlessness. "Kara, please say something."

With worry coating his tone, I instantly feel guilty. I don't mean to make him worry. Although I'm too ashamed to say it doesn't bother me all that much. I want him to suffer for being such a deceitful prick.

"Kara, say something." He makes his demand through the door, but again I continue to ignore him. Even though my heart is pleading for me to cave.

"Kara, say something. Yell at me, I don't care. Just say something."

"No!" I roll my eyes at the word that leaps from my

throat. *No?* Now he has proof that I'm not being rational. I groan into the pillow.

"Kara, I'm sorry." The handle jiggles and then he bangs his palm on the door again. "Open the door, treasure."

"Red!" I shout out the door. He doesn't get to call me treasure. He broke my trust. "I'm not your pet anymore." My heart beats so loud I imagine he can hear it.

I'm met with nothing but silence.

After a long moment. He finally speaks. "Kara, it's almost time for lunch." I roll my eyes. He can't lure me out of here with the promise of food. My mouth waters remembering this morning's meal. A good portion is still sitting on the tray at the foot of the bed. There's so much cured meat still piled on the tray, I'd probably be good for two or three days.

"Kara, I want to take you to lunch and have you meet some of the residents here. They're going to take you shopping." His words are laced with bribery. As if he can buy me pretty trinkets and clothes, and I would be all right with his deceit.

"Not going to happen!" I yell back in a sing song voice.

He bangs on the door again. "Damn it, Kara, open the door!"

"No!"

"Treasure, I'm going to punish your ass—"

I cut him off and almost open the damn door just so I can yell in his face. I race to the door and scream at it knowing he's on the other side. "I'm not your treasure! You don't get to have me anymore. Not when you lied to me!" I don't even attempt to censor myself. "You were just going to breed me and then what? You didn't seem too keen on me staying. Or were you just waiting to see if I could even have your…" The words die on my lips. That's exactly what he was doing. Tears brim and I let them come. He only wanted me if I could have his dragonlings. My hand flies to my lower belly as my lower lip drops.

"Kara, stop it. I know what you're thinking. It's not like that."

I don't even have the energy to respond. I walk slowly back to the bed.

"Kara!" he screams, but I don't answer. Not because I want to piss him off, just because I don't have anything to say back. I'm so bloody hurt. It's not at all about me or a mate or heat… it's about dragonlings.

He bangs for a while longer, yells and speaks calmly, he does everything he can to get me to open the door, but I lay on the bed feeling numb as it all turns to white noise.

So what if I'm not pregnant? Galen said my heat has passed. I could be pregnant now with his dragonlings. But I remember Victor talking about how hard it is for women to get pregnant. How it would take years of nurturing a mated relationship and dragons are impatient. I can't imagine I'd get pregnant on the first try.

"Kara, please open the door." He sounds both

exhausted and defeated. I only barely hear him through my thoughts. I feel used and spent. I don't want to fight. I only want to get out of here. I slip off the bed and turn the key in the lock.

"I'm surprised you didn't knock it down," I mutter as I turn away from the door and walk back to the bed. I don't get on it though; I stare at it as he talks.

"Kara, treasure." I turn to him with anger and give him a look to shut his mouth. His eyes widen at my anger, and he puts his hands up as if he's approaching a wild, wounded animal. "Kara, it's not what you think."

"How would you know what I'm thinking?"

"It's not hard to guess what you're assuming."

"Assuming? Okay here's what I'm *assuming*. I'm assuming that you were keeping me around until you figured out whether or not I'd be able to get pregnant for you." I pause thinking maybe I should tell him what the sorcerer said. Maybe I should fill him in on the fact that it takes years of mating and bonding before dragonlings are able to be carried by humans. But I decide not to. I don't want him to keep me around just to be tossed in a few years if I can't get pregnant. I feel more for him than I have anyone else, and I could see myself allowing this treatment if only he would pretend to love me. Feeling pathetic, I turn my back to him and close my eyes as if not seeing him will help how badly my heart hurts for what I know I must do. "I want to leave. I'm not staying with you."

"You are staying with me. Kara, I love you." I huff a semblance of a sad laugh at his words.

"You're only saying that because I was able to heat. I know how rare that is for you dragons."

"That's not true."

I point at the bathroom door behind us. "Only hours ago you couldn't give me a straight answer on how long you wanted to *keep me,*" I sneer the words remembering how much I wanted him to want me. "But now you love me?" I widen my eyes and force the tears to stay back. My chest feels like something is tearing at my heart and ripping it to shreds.

"I know it sounds bad." I turn away from him to gather something better to put on than this damn night-gown, but then I stop and press my lips together. I don't want anything from him. I'll just leave in this. Whatever. I'll find somewhere I can stay in exchange for work. I'll figure out something on my own. I always have. I survive. That's what I do.

I start walking to the door, but Drago stands in my way. "Move."

"You could be pregnant with my dragonlings. You will stay here."

"I'm not sleeping with you." He's lost his mind if he thinks that's happening.

"I'll leave; I don't have to stay in the same room." I'm surprised by how easily he backs down. "I see that you need space so I'm willing to give it to you. I will give you time to settle down and adjust."

"I'm leaving when you see I'm not pregnant."

A look of pure hurt crosses his face and I almost regret my words. *Almost.*

He reaches for my hand and takes the key from me. I give it up easily, making sure his skin doesn't touch mine, and I take a step back. I don't want him to touch me. His touch is a drug to me, a spell I wish I could break.

"I'm taking this though. There's no reason for you to lock the door."

"Why didn't you just break it down?" He looks at me with pain in his eyes.

"Sit down and I'll tell you."

"I don't care enough to obey you." I walk away from him to go wash my heated face down with cool water. I look back over my shoulder to add, "I'm not your pet anymore."

I have to admit I'm curious. But he doesn't get to command me anymore. I won't submit to someone I don't trust. To someone who was going to use me and spit me out when I didn't produce an heir for him. I'm all too aware how much he could hurt me. I wish he'd just do it, just show me the monster he is so I could stop feeling so much for him. That's going to hurt me in ways no beast can.

His footsteps are heard over the sound of the running water. My fingers slip beneath it, feeling how cool it is and waiting for it to warm just slightly.

His question is murmured. "Have you heard of the purge?" He sighs deeply as he takes a seat on the bench by the large soak-in tub that he bathed me in. Peeking over my shoulder, I'm caught in his gaze, which shines with grief and memories that never leave. I nod my head and swallow thickly.

"I've been told stories," I answer him. One dragon wanted all the wealth, all the power. He tricked the others into a gathering and decimated them. All but the three young dragons. It's rumored they possess a dangerous combination of magic. My body shudders as I remember how scared I was when I first walked into the throne room. To see the three of them, together. It's a truly intimidating sight.

"So you know how my uncle killed the other dragons and then tried to kill us?" I turn sharply at the counter to face him.

"Your uncle? That's awful. How could your own family betray you like that?"

"Yes, he was my uncle." With my back to the vanity, I grip the edge of it and watch Drago as he tells me the story. "My mother was a magic dragon, like Cyrus. She had the most beautiful green eyes. It's all I really remember about her." My heart aches for him, knowing how painful it can be to lose everyone in your life. Well almost everyone, save his brothers. At least I knew it was coming. I always had someone up until last week.

"She sealed the doors when the purge happened. She used the last of her strength to seal each of our doors with her magic." He isn't emotional speaking about it. But I can still feel his pain. "We listened to it. To their screams. It was over quickly, believe it or not. It can't have been more than minutes that passed." My eyes fall to the floor as I imagine such tragedy. I want to go to him and comfort him. But then I realize that's probably what he wants. Is he using this to get to me? To make me surrender and cave to him. I hate the feeling of betrayal that comes over me.

"With the key in the locks, no harm will come to those concealed by the doors." He looks past me to his bedchambers. "Luckily he wore himself out trying to get our doors open." He shakes his head. "My uncle was a brute but a coward." Anger fumes from him as his eyes flash red. "He was so tired from trying to get through the door he didn't see as Cyrus's magic lulled him to sleep. He was too afraid to call out to us and risk waking him though. So he stayed in his room listening to our uncle breathe on the other side of the door until Galen and I gathered up the strength to open our doors. I will never break down the door...it's all that's left of our mother."

"I'm sorry, Drago." My voice is hoarse and cracks at the end. He stands and makes a move to brush my cheek as my eyes turn glassy with tears, but I turn away from him. My heart aches worse than ever before, and at this point it could be a number of things causing the pain.

After a long moment of silence, he says, "I'll give you space, but you need to eat. I still want to feed you."

I don't bother trying to suppress the need to roll my eyes. "I'm not going to starve myself over you, Dr—" I'm stopped by his hand suddenly grabbing my chin.

"I'll give you space, treasure, because I know you need time right now. But watch your mouth, Kara." He leans down and steals a forceful kiss from me. His lips are like fire, and they burn a deep need inside of me. I'm breathless as he pulls back, my heart hammering at his brutal touch. "I'm keeping tabs of all your insolence."

He lets go of me and moves his hand away fast enough that I can't do a thing but attempt to regain my balance.

He scents the air and looks at me with a threat dancing in his eyes. My cheeks burn with embarrassment. I wish his threat didn't just send an intense wave of arousal to my core. "No pleasuring yourself, treasure." I part my lips but bite back my snide comment as his heated look meets mine. I glance down and see his hardened dick and then back up to him.

"So you can get yourself off all you want while I have to be in discomfort because you're a lying prick?" I huff out in anger. "You forgot, I'm not your pet to boss around anymore."

"Watch it treasure; you're really pushing me." His eyes spark red and I can practically feel his beast. I want to push him. I want him to hold me down like he did last night. I want him to punish me and own me. He takes a sharp inhale, sensing my need for him. I quickly close my eyes and turn back to the sink. Ignoring the sexual tension between us.

"I'll be back here for lunch."

"I already ate." It's a lie, but he can't know that. He

opens his mouth to question me but then he seems to remember the tray on the bed, and he literally curses under his breath. I bite back my smile.

"I'll see you for dinner then."

"Fine." I agree just so he'll leave me. But he stays and watches as I wash my face.

I pat my skin dry with a plush hand towel and catch his eyes in the mirror. "What?" I keep my tone even.

"I truly am sorry, Kara. And I do love you." I stare at him for a moment. I want to believe him, but I don't. There's no reason he should love me. He only loves that he thinks I could give him dragonlings.

I pace back to his bedchambers, walking around his large form. I say without looking back at him, "I'll see you at dinner, Drago."

CHAPTER 14

I KNOW NOTHING OF A LIFE OF WEALTH OR power. Nearly everything I think I know about dragons could be untrue. So much of my current reality evades me. But I am all too aware, as I sit in silk, that there is much to be grateful for. Even if he lied. Even if he only wishes to use me. This could be a life protected. Or at least a moment where I could truly rest without worry.

That's what I keep thinking. Drago saved my life. He's treated me better than I've ever expected. I love what he does to me in every way, physically. Even if I don't want to be lied to nor do I wish to be used. A very broken, beaten down part of me wants to submit and be grateful. An even more depraved part of me wants to tell him it could happen in a few years or more. That desperate piece of my soul hopes he'll give me his attention for that long if he believes it'll be possible to breed me.

I haven't moved from the grand bed and silence has left me with a mix of thoughts.

Most of them lead to one conclusion: if I stay, I will

fall for him beyond repair. He will have every bit of control, and a part of me craves nothing more than that. All the rest of me though, knows never to trust a dragon.

A loud bang of the door swinging open catches me off guard and has a scream of surprise tearing from my throat.

"My Lady, are you all right?" A young woman asks from the doorway. She's dressed like the others in a simple linen dress. Her long, dark hair is braided and put up in a perfect and tightly pinned back bun. Her skin is like porcelain and her eyes are the palest blue. I've never seen someone with such dark hair yet light eyes. She's young and lean, probably my age. She raises her brows in question and takes a step forward. "Are you all right, my Lady?"

I nod my head and my forehead pinches in confusion as I whisper my question. "Why are you calling me Lady?"

Her back straightens and her head bows as she clasps her hands in front of her and answers in a hushed tone. "We've been told to address you in that manner. Forgive me; please allow me to address you as you see fit. I need only to know what you prefer." She talks to the ground, and it makes my stomach twist in a knot.

"Stop it." I crawl off the bed and walk to her. She takes a step back like she's afraid of me. "You can call me whatever the hell you want to. My name is Kara, so I'd prefer that, but I've been known as *that bitch* before also so that works too. What else did he tell you?"

She looks up at me with bewildered eyes. "M—" She clears her throat. "Kara?"

"Yes?"

"You'd prefer for us to call you Kara?" she asks as though she doesn't understand the simple normalcy.

"That's my name. What's yours?" I ask.

"Zinnea," she answers.

"Oh, that's pretty. Like a flower." She blushes and smiles sweetly before returning her gaze to the floor.

"Stop looking at the floor please. You can look at me like anyone else. I'm not a Lady."

"Lord Arrington has informed us that you are his mate, and you are to be treated as such."

A warmth spreads over me but I don't trust it. The young woman stares back to me, waiting for my response. "I'm not certain that's true."

Her eyes widen. "You don't wish to be with him?"

I look behind her into the hall before asking, and completely ignoring her question, "Where do you go for privacy?"

"In the den mostly."

"Could we go there, or anywhere else that's not this room?" I ask her.

"Yes, I could give you a tour of sorts, if you'd like?"

"Please. Let me change first and then I'd like to get out of this room." I turn to go to the pile of clothes and breathe deeply. The jewelry is in boxes next to it and that reminds me of the collar on my neck. I fiddle with the clasp in the back, but I can't get it.

"Zinnea?" I ask as I turn to her, "would you please unhook this for me?"

"Your collar?"

"Yes," I answer. "I can't get it."

"M—" she corrects herself. "I'm afraid that Lord Arrington will be extremely displeased if his collar was removed by anyone other than himself."

I whip my head around. "Excuse me?"

"It's his and it being on you is a symbol that you're his. Taking it off would be akin to taking you away from him."

I stare at her for a minute, feeling my heart sink. I swallow and reach around to fiddle with the clasp again. The chain falls the moment the clasp is free, and it drops to a puddle in my hand. I leave it on the dresser and make my way to the clothes. It takes me a moment to realize she hasn't followed. When I turn around, Zinnea is staring at the table I've left the collar on with wide eyes and her mouth open in shock.

With a heavy exhale, I decide to keep this night dress on. I don't want to wear anything else he picked out for me or any of these expensive clothes. I'd rather wear the linen dress Zinnea is wearing.

"Can we go now?" I'm ready to get the hell out of this room and get this fog in my head cleared. I'm hopeful that the farther I can get away from Drago, the clearer I'll be able to think.

Zinnea swallows and nods, although she seems a shade paler than before. She leads the way down the long hall. With the daylight it's so much easier to see than it was the night before. The windows are floor to ceiling and line the hall on the right. The left side has large paintings that I wasn't quite able to make out last night. I shudder remembering what happened after. Thankfully, Zinnea distracts me with a question.

"Are you cold?"

I shake my head no. "I would like to wear something else though."

"Are we going shopping?" Zinnea's blue eyes light with happiness, and a large smile forms on her face. I take it she enjoys shopping.

"I don't have any money at the moment." She looks me up and down with a frown and opens her mouth but closes it.

"Let's go to the kitchen and get some sweets." She leads me down a narrower hall with no windows that's lit with torches.

"What's with all the torches?" I have to ask. There's electric and running water yet these torches are everywhere.

"For tradition. The Lords like to keep certain things as they were when they were young." She leans in close and whispers, "Before their parents passed." She pushes the double doors open to a huge kitchen. It's complete with every possible commercial appliance there is available. It's all stainless steel and sterile. The light reflecting off the metal is nearly blinding.

I nod in understanding. "It was so long ago though. So much has changed."

"In many ways yes, but in many ways nothing has changed." Mrs. Sarah answers from her position at the sink. I stop in my tracks and watch as Zinnea skips over to her.

"How many sweets would you like?" I don't even realize Zinnea is talking to me until both women look back and stare at me.

"Just one, please."

Zinnea looks back at me with a look of disbelief and then climbs on a stool to get to an upper cabinet. "One of each it is," she says cheerfully before climbing down with a handful of brightly colored candies. "Mrs. Sarah, we'll need a little bowl if you have one."

The older woman smirks at her. "You'll need a bowl Zinni. Don't blame this on our Lady of the castle."

"Her name is Kara. And she doesn't want to be called Lady." Zinnea sits on the counter swinging her legs and looks back to me as she keeps talking to Mrs. Sarah. She says in a hushed tone, "I thought you may want to talk to her some. She also says she has no money to go shopping." I don't miss her raised brow and knowing look she gives the older woman before glancing back at me.

"Oh, dear." The older woman looks at me from head to toe, her lips pursed. Suddenly my throat goes dry. With a quizzical look she comments, "But you love him."

My heart sputters in my chest. I shake my head no,

but really I'm not sure it's the truth. And I'm not a liar. I spear my fingers through my hair. "I don't know."

Mrs. Sarah walks to the fridge with a sigh, ignoring my response, and pulls out a bowl of peeled shrimp and places it on the counter. All the while I watch and wait, as if this woman's opinion would mean anything at all. She digs back in the fridge and sighs, pulling out a bowl of shrimp shells. I suppose she's making a broth. I try to convince myself that what anyone else thinks is irrelevant, but for some reason, I can't. I'm desperate for someone else to explain what I feel to me. I'm at a complete loss—torn, confused, and on the verge of admitting that I am in love, although none of it feels as if it's in my control.

"I bet you do know," she says matter of factly, interrupting my thoughts, as she grabs a pot hanging over the stainless-steel counter. Ignoring my racing heart, I purse my lips and consider her words as she fills the pot with water and sets it on the stove.

"I don't trust how I feel." Again, I settle on the truth.

"Ah!" She holds her finger up. "You're afraid."

"No." I respond instantly. I am *never* afraid.

Turning to look over her shoulder, Mrs. Sarah smirks at me, wiping her hands on her apron. "Of course you're afraid. Everyone is afraid when they're in love."

As she turns her attention back to the pot, I murmur, half wishing I could keep my thoughts to myself, "I don't want to feel this way."

"Which way is that? In love or afraid?" she questions,

her back still to me as if this is a casual conversation. Swallowing thickly, I glance to my right at Zinnea and expect to find her leaning over and ready to pounce on my insecurities, but she's simply unwrapping a sweet and popping it into her mouth.

"I don't know which is worse." The truth in my statement is unsettling.

"The worst thing that could happen is that you give him your heart and he breaks it." She grabs a few peppers and onions and chops them with ease as she adds, "And I have a feeling Drago wouldn't do anything to hurt you, Kara."

I almost tell her he lied to me. I almost tell her I don't know that I trust myself around him. Instead I just say straight to the point, "I may be pregnant with his dragonlings." I don't need to explain that matters would get far more complicated if I am pregnant. I grip the edge of the counter a little tighter as Zinnea unwraps another sweet, pretending not to be listening but I'm all too aware she is.

There's no judgment at all in Mrs. Sarah's response. She doesn't stop her knife or the chopping. "He should be able to scent by now. It's nearly instant for dragons."

"How instant?" I ask, my neck and cheeks heating.

"Within hours of your heat leaving you, you would smell of pregnancy." The vegetables drop into the pot, and she busies herself cleaning the cutting board.

As my insecurities and a million questions race in my mind, I ask her, "Do you smell it?"

"Sweetheart, I'm just a human. You'd have to ask a

dragon that. And seeing as how your Drago is the only dragon around right now, maybe you should ask him."

"Where are his brothers?" I question. "Cyrus and Galen?"

"They should be back by night fall." She takes in a nervous breath. "They've gone to see about acquiring someone." A shudder runs through her body.

"You're worried?" I ask.

Her eyes find mine. "A bit. I'm sure they'll be careful, but what they're doing could"—she hesitates before saying—"add complications."

A chill runs down my shoulders. I look at the exit to the kitchen and wonder where Drago is.

"Let's go Kara," Zinnea says with an upbeat voice as she hops off the counter. "It's time to go shopping." I watch as she pockets more sweets and winks at me. Well, if nothing else, it'll give me a distraction and get me out of here.

CHAPTER 15

I SCENT THE AIR AS SOON AS I GET TO THE DINING hall. But the scent of her heat is long gone, and the scent of her pregnancy doesn't exist. *It didn't happen.* My throat runs dry and my heart sinks. As I take another step, I know in my soul that it's true. I'd be able to scent her pregnancy by now. She's not carrying my dragonlings.

With every hollow step I take, my brother's warning comes back to me. She'll more than likely never heat again so long as she's in my presence. The door groans as I open it and I do everything in my power not to show the emotions that riddle their way through me. I'd hoped for dragonlings with her and a future that would carry a legacy. The moment my gaze meets hers, all thoughts of what I once hoped for are quieted. Looking into her gorgeous hazel eyes, a smile plays at my lips and a pull I can't control soothes my worries. It appears my feelings are one-sided, however. Her eyes are narrowed and her mouth is pursed as she sits at a high table in the corner of the bedroom. Her little ass is still mad. Although it's sexy as hell, I'm ready for her to be my little pet again. I love her fight; I love her submission to me even more. As the door closes with a resounding click, I decide I will gain her forgiveness if it's the last thing I do.

She's the greatest treasure I've ever had. I won't let her go.

In front of her is an empty plate with some sort of sauce smeared and tiny bits of broccoli left over. She already ate. Without me.

"How was dinner?" I ask as sarcastically as I can. She has the decency to at least drop her gaze in what appears to be guilt before lifting her head once again and answering.

"Delicious." She twists her fingers nervously but gives me hard eyes as she says, "I spent some of your money as well. I needed normal clothing." She doesn't keep eye contact and I know she isn't comfortable with it. But I'm pleased she did. Every step I take toward her is cautious.

"Good." It's then that I see she's in a simple, pale pink dress. She'd look stunning in anything she wore. "You look beautiful. I'm glad you were able to find some things to your taste here." The tension in the air between us is thick. Kara tenses her shoulders and I'm not sure if it's because she didn't enjoy the trip or because I'm getting closer to her. My eyes travel to her neck.

She took off her collar. My body heats with a sense of anger, but also something else. *Loss.* Fuck, that hurts.

My dragon stirs with fire, and I have to pause, uncertain of what to do.

"Did you have a nice time?" I ask, to focus on anything other than the fact that she took off her collar. She'll be my pet again and begging for my forgiveness as she comes undone on my cock. The thought is calming. I'll bide my time until then.

"Can you smell anything?" she asks with a clipped tone, staring past me at the closed door. It's all too obvious she's planning to leave. No dragonlings. No mate. No Kara.

I won't allow it. I take another step toward her. "Sorry, my treasure. I can't tell yet." I lie to her. I'll lie for as long as I can so that I can keep her.

"You said it would only take a few days." Her voice is laced with irritation.

A lump rises in my throat; I hate that she wants to leave me.

I don't answer her and I don't have to. She continues speaking. "I heard the women talking. Galen and Cyrus left." She finally looks back at me with concern rather than anger. "You're going to go to war with Victor, aren't you?"

I shake my head. "There's no need to start a war. Galen merely wants an opportunity to court someone they're hiding from us."

"But why?" she questions, genuinely interested but also concerned. "I don't understand why they would do that. Why keep someone from you?" My treasure looks back at me with confusion but also with need for answers. It's better than the alternative—her silence, her disobedience, her desire to leave—so I nurture her curiosity.

"I'm not sure. It could be to end our line. We are the most powerful shifters. I don't know why they'd risk it though... There's no other reason that she would be there that I can think of." She stares into my eyes as if she'll find an answer there. I wish I could give her one. I truly do. "Had I not seen her lineage myself, I would think she didn't exist, and that Victor was merely toying with us." Anger fumes inside of me at his name on my lips. Once again, my dragon stirs, eager to protect Kara from ever again being harmed.

"So you're siding with Victor if this ends in war?" The worry in her voice gives her a broken cadence. I hate that she's worrying, but I love that she's concerned for us.

"No." I nearly whisper as I finally reach the high table. Her wide eyes stay locked with mine. "We will fight against the Authority if they try to take what's ours. That is not the same." I squat down next to her chair to be eye level with Kara. "I'll be killing Victor myself." Ever so gently, I push the hair out of her face and tuck it behind her ear. My thumb brushes along her cheek. "I will kill him for what he's done to you."

She doesn't pull away from my touch. *Progress.*

"Thank you." Her voice is small and melancholy. "I wish you wouldn't lie to me."

"I didn't lie to you." My heart skips in my chest. "I'll

bring his head to you if that's what you want." My solemn words are spoken with every bit of sincerity I have in me.

Her hazel eyes stare back at me. "I'm not pregnant, Drago." Her jaw is squared and her teeth clenched. She's putting on a mask. It's all too obvious she's holding back tears.

I attempt to gather an excuse but she cuts me off. "The women were talking, Drago. I know you know. Stop lying to me."

Fuck. Fire burns in the depths of me and urges me to make this right. "It's all right, we can try again, but the odds—" the look in her eyes keeps me from finishing. A concoction of sadness and rage stares back at me.

She shakes her head. No. No. My heart races. I can't let her go. "So I can't give you dragonlings?" she asks with no emotion other than contempt.

"I don't think you can," I answer simply and truthfully, knowing I need her to stay. Quietly, I sit in the seat next to her with my hand on the table. Palm up. I wait for her to hold my hand. But she doesn't. Instead she stares at it.

"Then why do you even want me here?" she asks, not bothering to look at me.

"I told you. I love you, Kara."

"Until you find someone to carry your young."

I shake my head in disgust. "There is no one else for me!"

She accuses, "You'll only keep me as a pet until you

find someone else." She continues to speak without looking at me, staring across the room at nothing.

"Is that what you've convinced yourself? What have I ever done to give you that impression?"

"You only wanted to breed me," she answers with a flat tone, and I can feel her slipping away. I wish she were angry. I don't like the lack of emotion from her. I need her passion, even if it's because she's angry. This is like she's given up. Given up on us. My dragon rages inside of me to be let out. Even that side of me has lost faith in my abilities to keep her.

She must feel this pull, this fire between us. How can she not? Is it because she's only human?

"That's not true, Kara. I was drawn to you before I scented you. I was trying to wait to fuck you." I swallow the harsh emotions and keep my dragon at bay. "This is exactly why. I knew you would get the wrong idea," I say as she shakes her head in anger. "Don't deny my feelings for you. You deny your own all you want. But I love you and I know that you love me as well."

She rises from the table so quickly the chair nearly topples, brushing away tears from her eyes. I rise with her, and my chair does fall but I ignore it.

"Where are you going?" I ask as she turns her back to me and storms off. My heart races and my blood chills. I'm caught between the desperate need to forcibly keep her here and the reality of what harm that would cause.

"I need to go think."

"What's there to think about?" I ask to her back as she stalks toward the doorway, away from me yet again.

"What I want," she says simply, although her voice is tight with tension.

"You know what you want," I press.

She turns violently, her face flushed and her eyes wide as she yells, "I have no fucking clue what I want!" With anger in her steps, she closes the distance between us and her voice cracks. "I've never wanted anything in my life other than to escape death for as long as I could and have vengeance for those who've hurt me and my family."

I press down the anger rising in my chest at the thought of someone hurting her. "I've never had the chance to want for anything. Never had a chance to even consider what I *wanted*. I wasn't born into luxury and power!" She practically spits the last line. I can't help that I was born into wealth and power. Her eyes brim with tears and I hate that this is how we came to be. If only I could have saved her long ago. If only I could go back.

I have compassion and empathy, but I do not have leniency for how she speaks to me.

She is mine. My submissive, and her behavior will be dealt with.

I allow her to step closer, so close I can feel her heat, as she stomps toward me with a finger pointed at my chest, her lips parted to continue her display of rage, but she is stopped by my response. I scoop her ass up with one hand, squeezing that lush flesh. My cock hard and my primal need begging me to give her what she truly needs. It happens in a blur while my need to remind her who she is to me and what I can give her fuels me. I grab both the hands she sends flying to my chest and pin her wrists above her head as I push her back into the wall. Her body is hot against mine and does nothing to tame the beast inside of me. She screams out and struggles against me until I press my body against her.

"Don't fucking hate me for something I can't control, Kara." Her breasts rise and fall as she takes in heavy breaths. With my lips parted slightly, I kiss her neck and wait for her to say it, but I pray she doesn't. It fucking kills me that her neck is bare. I drag my lips up as my heart pounds against hers. She should be wearing my collar.

Mine. The possessiveness whispers in the back of my mind as she stills in my grasp.

She's safeworded me every time since Galen's tattled on me. Every time I put my hands on her, she's safeworded me.

Hope kindles the fire between us as I kiss her neck again and feel her arch her back, letting out a feminine sigh of desire.

I murmur against the shell of her ear, "Is that the way to speak to your Dom?" Chills flow down her shoulder and she shudders with desire. I pull back to look into her eyes. Her hazel eyes flash with desperate need.

I know she wants this. I know she wants me. Although I wait for that one word to be uttered from her lips. Please don't say it, my love.

She doesn't answer me and I'm not sure how much to push her. I nip her jaw and then her earlobe. My cock jumps as she lets out a small moan and her head falls back against the wall.

"You need to be punished for talking to me like that."

She swallows thickly with her eyes closed and then looks back at me to answer, "I'm sorry, Sir." I repress my groan.

"Sorry isn't good enough." I lean in and whisper into her ear, letting my warm breath tickle her neck. "Especially when you took your collar off. My naughty little pet."

The sweet smell of her arousal hits me, and I don't even fucking care that a shudder goes through my body and a groan tears through my throat.

"You need to be spanked for your disrespect."

When I open my eyes, she's looking back at me with a hint of a smile. Her little hand comes up and cups my chin, "You really love me, Drago?" There's doubt in her eyes.

"I do, my treasure. I love you, Kara." I almost tell her she must be my mate, but I haven't a way to know it. There is only lore and none of it ever suggested a human could mate with a dragon.

Her simper turns doleful, and I can tell she doesn't believe me. It crushes me that she doubts what I tell her. But how could she not when I've lied to her before?

"Punish me, Drago." Her sultry words slip between her lips as she kisses me with the heated passion I've missed. My dragon purrs inside of me, rubbing against my chest, loving the feel of her body on mine.

Quickly, I push my hand between her legs and feel the thin fabric shielding her core from me. I tear the lace easily and toss it to the ground. My lips are still on hers and I silence her gasp as I kiss her harder and play with her cunt. I test her, running my fingers up her slick folds all the way up her clit, which I give special attention. Every little movement from Kara is needy. She arches her back and presses herself into me. She's fucking addictive. I groan into her mouth.

"So wet for your mate. You're such a good girl." Her head falls back against the wall as I push two fingers into her tight, welcoming heat. *Fuck*, she's so tight. My cock hardens impossibly so. I curl my fingers and massage her g-spot. I watch in awe as her lips part and her breath comes in pants. A blush travels up her chest and into her cheeks. Fucking gorgeous. She swallows and moans as her body trembles ever so slightly. She's so close.

All of a sudden, her head shoots forward and her eyes plead with me. "Don't Drago, please." I'm caught off guard. I instantly still inside her.

"What happened my treasure?" I'm careful with my words although my blood is scorching and my need barely contained. "What did I do? I won't do it again."

Tears well in her eyes and she swallows thickly. "I'm sorry Drago. Please don't punish me like this again."

Relief is instant as it hits me. She's terrified I'll deny her again. That's what she doesn't want me to do. With a smirk barely hidden, I kiss her and silence her pleas. I slip my hand from her heat and quickly shove my pants down to get my length lined up. As soon as I'm there I grab her hip to keep her steady and thrust into her heat. It's a merciless single stroke. My mouth stays on hers, trapping her strangled cry. I pull out slowly and fuck back into her.

As my pace picks up, her nails dig into my shoulders and it's then I give her all of me.

"I'll punish you later treasure; right now, I need you."

As a reward, she moans my name.

I leave open-mouthed kisses down her throat and run my teeth along her collar bone. She shudders under me and pushes her heels into my ass as I keep my steady rhythm.

She goes off beneath me, crying out my name once again as her tight walls pulse around my dick. Pushing her dress farther up, my hand moves to her clit and rubs along the sides of the throbbing nub. I want another one. I need her overwhelmed with pleasure. I rut into her as she trembles with her orgasm, riding through it as my own pleasure rises. She finally gasps for air and her hands fly to my jaw. She kisses me like she needs my lips on hers in order to breathe. My hand wraps around her neck as I keep fucking into her and kissing her with the same desperation.

I pull back as I feel her pussy tense up again. She bites her lip as she keeps her eyes on mine. I stare into her hazel eyes as I pound into her pussy—once, twice, three more times until we both find our release in unison. I catch her moans with my kiss and hold her tight to me until both of our orgasms have passed. Even then I hold her in my arms and just enjoy the feel of her against me.

After a moment she rests her head, still catching her breath, on my shoulder and kisses my neck. She wraps her arms around my back and settles against my chest. It warms my heart. I lift her up and cradle her body to take her to bed. I look down at my little treasure and she gives me a small, sweet smile and runs her hand along my chin.

She may not believe that I love her.

But I know she loves me.

CHAPTER 16

HIS SCENT SURROUNDS ME AS DOES HIS warmth. I've never felt so comfortable, so relaxed, so very much like I'm in the one place I'm meant to be. So safe…so cherished. I nuzzle into Drago's chest as he settles us into bed.

Part of me doesn't trust it. I think about fighting him. About keeping up my walls, but it's so damn exhausting. I want to be free with him and have this feeling forever. I've never felt more *me* than when I'm with him. I don't know whether I'll ever truly believe that he loves me. It's possible I'll always question that he only wants me for the possibility of having dragonlings. Is that so bad though? If I'm happy? Can't I just pretend that I believe him? I want to so badly. I want to believe that this pull I have deep inside my chest to be close to him and to open myself up to him is felt by him too. With the nagging thoughts refusing to give me peace, I peer up through my thick lashes and find him staring at me.

"Treasure." He leans down to kiss me and takes my jaw in his hand. Hearing that name on his lips sounding like devotion breaks my last wall. I crumble beneath his touch. He nips my bottom lip and then suckles it. I smile as he pulls away from me. He keeps his hand on my chin and then rests his forehead on mine with his eyes closed.

His deep masculine voice is only a murmur as he commands, "Tell me you believe me, Kara."

"That I believe what?" I ask although I'm all too aware.

"That you believe I love you."

Before I can answer him, a commotion comes from somewhere in the castle: a deadly scream and one filled with terror. A chill runs through my body as the two of us jump from where we are, both of us staring at the door as if it would tell us what happened just now.

"Stay," Drago commands me and I look at him like he's lost his mind. "Behind me." He acts like he's just finishing his sentence. He swallows thickly as he climbs from bed and dresses quickly.

I do as he says, all the while my heart races.

All the comfort I felt vanishes as we walk quickly down the hall to the wide spiral staircase. My bare feet pad on the cold stone floor. The noises of people gasping and the shifters yelling orders grow louder and louder.

I remember the worry in Mrs. Sarah's comment, and it strikes me that Drago's brothers may not have come back alone. My grip is clammy on the iron railing of the staircase as I peek over the banister and see

Cyrus is on the ground and has a death grip on his leg. He's naked, so he obviously just shifted. As we get closer, I smell charred flesh and it nearly makes me gag. Cyrus's leg is blackened and bloodied. It all comes into view as if it's slow motion. Galen hovers over him and behind both of them is what appears to be a large canvas bag with a drawstring top. It could easily fit a body and judging by the muffled cries coming from it and the movement within it, that's exactly what it contains.

Holy fuck. My hand flies to my mouth as I stay where I am on the staircase. Numbly, I stand dumbfounded watching the scene play out before me. My legs lock and Drago leaves me near the top of the stairs as he marches downward to figure out what the hell is going on.

"What happened?" Drago's demand is hard although concern is etched on his face. A healer, draped in deep burgundy, wipes away the blood from Cyrus's leg and speaks spells I've never heard to numb the pain. Servants fill the room slowly but keep their distance. They all watch with terror filled eyes. No one dares to speak.

"The sorcerer saw us." Galen's voice is calm although his chest is heaving. Even from here I can see he's covered in sweat from head to toe. A servant scuttles forward with his head bowed to pass Galen his clothes and then leans down to hand Cyrus the same. Galen takes the clothes with one hand and nods in thanks before heaving in a ragged breath and shoving a leg into the pants.

They've just come back. From the Authority. The weight of the realization makes my chest hurt. *Isabella.* My eyes refuse to leave the bag.

"Did they follow you?" Drago's eyes narrow before he takes a quick glance at me. His fear and tension are palpable but quickly extinguished when both Cyrus and Galen shake their heads no.

"Alec tried. We were almost out with no one even knowing," Cyrus answers, his voice quieting as he glances down at his leg.

"One of the women screamed and called for Alec." Galen walks to the bag, his footsteps foreboding. Unconsciously I take a step back, seeing the side of the bag, pierced and soaked in dark red. *A talon. Blood.* I attempt to take another step back, but I can't. As if simply not seeing would make it all go away.

"He got me pretty good. But we got them," Cyrus continues with a tight smile, although he winces as the healer removes pieces of his charred skin. His gruff groan echoes his pain throughout the hall. He waves the healer away and inhales deeply before blowing out a dusting of green through the air. The green fog seems to sparkle as it fades in the air and falls onto his leg. My vision is blocked as more and more servants gather below, hovering around the scene.

"What do you mean you got them? I thought there was only one?" Drago questions them. Looking between the two before his eyes settle on the large canvas sack.

"I didn't know which one was Isabella." Galen opens the bag and two women, gagged and bound at the ankles, knees, and wrists, fall out. Only one woman is alive and struggling. The other woman is limp, and her chest is still. Her eyes are closed, but her skin is so pale it is nearly gray. As she lands on the cold, hard ground, blood smears on the ground and pools around her.

My entire body goes cold.

A high-pitched scream fills the space as my eyes widen and my knees go weak. I barely register that the sound is coming from me. They killed her. Several servants come to help me but I push them all away. I can't get the image of her falling lifeless to the floor out of my head. My hands clasp over my mouth as I shake my head in denial.

"Help her!" Galen screams. All three men crowd around the two women on the floor. A servant gets between them and pulls the woman who's alive and screaming through the gag away from the other. The poor young woman is hysterical and frantically trying to get free.

"Come with me dear." I almost shove against the small woman leading me away. But then I see her pale blue eyes pleading with me. Screams carry through the room. Yelling and shouting; several healers run into the room. I cry into Mrs. Sarah's arms as she walks me back to Drago's bedchambers.

I can hear them trying to save her, shouting at one another, but it all turns to white noise. How can you save someone who's already gone?

With my heart unable to stop racing, I pace the front of the door holding onto my crossed arms. I'm fucking freezing. I swallow the lump growing in my throat. At least I'm alive. Tears leak out of the corners of my eyes. I can't close them, when I do, I see her.

"She'll be all right dear." I stare at Mrs. Sarah, who has made herself at home in the bedroom, with disbelief and even a sense of betrayal. They killed her.

"How can you say that?" I'm barely able to speak with my throat being so dry and closed.

She stops rocking and looks at me with the sincerest eyes. "Because I know she'll be alright. Did you see her? Really see her?"

"Yes!" I scream and then regret yelling. My hands fist in my hair. "I can't stop seeing her."

"She was frozen, dear. Galen merely froze her. She'll be all right." I look back at her with wide eyes and then shake my head in disbelief.

"No she was bleeding."

"He froze her, dear. She can still be injured," she explains. "I'm sure he froze her before they left. To keep her quiet maybe? I'm not sure why. But she was only frozen not dead. It may seem as though she has lost her life, but I assure you my dear, Drago will walk through those doors any minute now and confirm what I'm telling you."

"Then why were they screaming?" I ask.

Her eyes narrow at me as if it's obvious. "She was hurt." The sound of the door opening startles me; I jump away from it and then see Drago and I run straight into his chest, wrapping my arms around him.

"There, there, treasure. Everything's all right."

I pull away from him and search his face for the truth. In a whisper, I ask, "Is she dead?"

"She's alive. I'm sorry you had to see that. She's all right now. Cyrus has healed her cut. I'm not sure he'll ever forgive himself, but Taryn will be just fine."

"Taryn?"

He gives me a tight smile and then leaves me to walk to the bathroom as he says under his breath, "Yes Taryn."

Mrs. Sarah takes that as her cue to get the hell out and I don't blame her. Drago runs his hands through his hair.

"What happened?" I question as Mrs. Sarah closes the door behind me and I slowly make my way to Drago. He's hunched over the sink, the faucet running. His eyes shine with so much emotion it's hard to know what he's thinking.

"Drago," I repeat, daring to get closer to him. "What happened?"

Tilting his head, he looks back at me and heaves in a deep breath as if he doesn't want to tell me. He runs a hand down his face before he speaks. "When they got there, they found Taryn and Isabella together and decided to take them both because they were both in heat."

"In heat?" I question and a new fear slows my pulse.

"Yes."

"Like I was?" I ask him and once again pull my arms over my chest.

"Yes," he answers and then stands up straighter.

"My brothers offered me the chance to court them, and I swear I said no, treasure. I told them you were my mate." He shakes his head, his eyes closed and his hands on his temples. "I actually punched Galen in the jaw for asking me. He knows I chose you as my mate and he had the fucking balls to question it."

Relief is instant as my heart swells.

"You told them I'm your mate?" I ask him although I know that's exactly what he just said.

"Yes," he answers me, and I can't help the smile that breaks across my face.

"So even though I can't give you dragonlings, you still want me?"

"Of course." He smiles the sexiest grin I've ever

seen as he walks toward me and wraps his arms around my waist. "I told you I love you."

I look up at him to ask, "Is she really okay?"

"Health wise they're fine." He swallows down whatever else he was going to say, and I can only imagine. His brothers kidnapped them. Injured them. And now they're locked away in a strange castle by magical beasts.

"Before you say anything, I want you to stay out of it," Drago tells me, and my eyes drop to the floor and then come back to his.

With his eyes piercing mine, he tells me, "There are things you do not understand."

"Then make me understand."

His hardened expression cracks and a smirk shows itself. "I intend to, but until then, stay away from my brothers and the women."

With a single nod, I reluctantly agree...for now.

EPILOGUE

KARA

Three Years Later

"H**MMM**." **D**ROWSILY, I **LIFT MY EYES AS** Drago's hand runs down my swollen belly. A soft smile plays at my lips. Stretching in the warmth of our bed I murmur, "Good morning, my love."

"Morning, my treasure." The bed groans as he leans over and kisses my neck, that sensitive spot just under my ear, and then my belly and the love in his action makes my body lean into him, wanting more. I spend each and every day craving his touch and I've never felt so complete.

With his touch, desire coils and I scissor my legs feeling a low burning need spiraling in my core. A rumble of approval purrs from his plump lips as he hovers his body over mine. His forearms rest on either side of my head as he leans down to kiss me. I part my legs and wrap them around him. My heels dig into his ass and try to push him toward me.

He resists.

I pout as prettily as I can. "Drago, I need you." I bat my eyes and lift my shoulders up so I can give him a quick kiss. His low, rough chuckle ignites the flames buried deep within me. I say his name like a plea, "Drago."

"What is it that you need?"

"You know." I nip his bottom lip and lower my voice. "You know exactly what I need."

He rocks his already hard erection into my heat and pulls back again. "You're damn right I know what you need." He leans down and whispers into my ear. His warm breath sends shivers down my body, hardening my nipples and sending a wave of arousal between my legs. "I want to hear you beg me to fuck you."

I don't even hesitate. "Drago, please." I stare into his dark eyes. "Please Drago, fuck me and make me yours in every way." I'm rewarded with the sexiest groan I've ever heard as he buries his head in my neck and rocks himself into me again.

The thin lace between us is shredded instantly. He tosses the scrap of material to the floor. I don't even know why I bother. His thick fingers dip into me as he pulls back and stares into my eyes. "That's my good girl." He puts his finger into his mouth and sucks. My head falls back against the pillow as his eyes slowly close and he groans that sexy fucking sound again.

He slowly sinks into me, his wide girth stretching my walls. My back bows as I gasp from his size. Fuck, I'll never get accustomed to him. He seems to know what

I'm thinking. A sexy grin forms on his face as he pushes himself in to the hilt and stills.

"So fucking good." He licks up my neck and nips my chin. His hands grip my hips, and he tilts me and holds me right where he wants me as pulls out slowly and pushes himself all the way to the hilt. There's slight relief as he pulls out, but my body begs for more. "Maybe I should make you come like this." My eyes fly open as he continues to tease me. "I'll fuck you deep and slow." I shake my head. I want him hard and deep. I want that primal desire in his eyes as he loses himself and fucks me like he owns me.

"I want my beast of a mate."

Drago chuckles, deep and masculine, as he pulls out. He stares between us, watching his dick move in and out with nothing but lust in his eyes. His lips part and his breaths come in short pants as he stills deep inside of me. My body writhes beneath him, wanting to move away from the intense pleasure, but needing more. I wish he'd fuck me like I'm used to. I need to come. Each slow thrust brings me closer. Yet I'm so far away.

"Please Drago." The words fall out of my mouth easily and without consent.

"Please what?" I smile at his question and then moan into the air as he pushes himself into me again. My back bows again and my head tilts and pushes into the mattress.

"Please make me come." I can barely breathe the words.

"I am." If I had the energy, I'd smack him. Instead I'm useless as my fists clench the sheets and my nails dig in, desperately hanging on to the edge of the cliff.

"Please Drago!" He pulls out slowly and I finally breathe out a breath I didn't know I was holding. While I have the opportunity, I dig my nails into his arms and pull myself up to kiss him. My tongue dives into his mouth. Our warm breath mingles and our tongues massage one another. He groans deep and low. "Please fuck me Drago. Hard, Drago. Be rough with me." It's not the first time I've had to beg him. Ever since I've become pregnant with his young, he's been gentler. But if I beg him, he gives me exactly what I need. And right now, I need the beast I've grown to love.

He slams into me as the last word leaves my lips, making me fall backward, and pumps into me with primal need. My body thrashes as a tingling heat pulses through me. He squeezes my ass as he continues his assault and my body arches and freezes. The sweet sting of my orgasm flows through me in merciless waves. Each one greater than the next. Hitting me fast and hard. My mouth drops open in ecstasy as he pounds into me over and over again. He doesn't let up, he fucks me as my release rips through me and takes me to a higher pleasure, drawing out my orgasm. My body trembles beneath me as he finds his release. He fucks into me with short, shallow thrusts until he's spent.

His body collapses next to mine and he pulls me into his chest. He kisses my hair and then my neck. I'm left feeling complete and satisfied. I yawn; I'm so fucking tired. Drago chuckles at me while my hand covers my mouth.

"Are you planning to sleep all day, my treasure?" As Drago asks, we hear the low pitter-patter of small feet coming toward our door.

"Put your clothes on!" Drago hisses as quietly as he can as my niece's tiny fist knocks at the door.

"Where is my night dress?" I question in a hushed tone. I can't find it anywhere. I throw the covers off the bed searching for it, but I can't find it anywhere.

"Here." Drago throws the pink cotton pajamas at me, and I scramble to put them on.

"Auntie Araaaaa." I smile as the little dragonling calls for me on the other side of the wall. I hop off the bed and run to the door. The key still stays on the table, but we no longer lock it every night. Maybe we should though.

"Cady!" I squeal as I open the door and scoop her up in my arms. Very much breathless with my heart pounding from almost being caught.

"Auntie Ara!" She claps her tiny little hands and then hugs me, putting her head on my chest. Her chubby little cheek is squished, making her look that much more adorable. She looks just like her father. She even has his eyes. Her hair is adorable done up in pigtails.

"Is it breakfast time already?" I ask the sweet little girl. She puts her thumb in her mouth and nods, going limp against me. Drago comes up beside us as we walk out of the bedchambers. He has my collar in his right hand and I stop in my tracks and arch my neck so he can put it on me. I love wearing it. I love being marked as his.

He moves my hair off my neck and clasps it in place. "Everyone knows who I belong to, Drago," I say as if I'm tsking him. I feel obligated to give him a hard time over the collar even if I smile all the while. He kisses me right above the collar on my neck and Cady pushes her little hand on his nose to push him away.

"Looks like it's nap time," he whispers to me.

"No!" Cady shoots up with wide, very much awake, eyes and shakes her head. I can't help but laugh as Drago throws his hands up in surrender.

If how he's been as an uncle is any indication of how he'll be as a father, then our children will be blessed. Tears prick at my eyes thinking soon we'll have our own. I never thought I'd be this happy. I didn't think happily ever afters existed. But they do. They really do.

The End…. or is it?

DRAGON'S SPELL

Alec

At the Estate of the Authority

"They've taken her." I'm out of breath. Sweat coats my body as the adrenaline rushes through my veins. My legs throb with pain from running through the field. My throat is hoarse from screaming. I shot everything I had at them. I couldn't hit them.

My Isabella. I couldn't risk hitting her, and I failed.

My chest collapses on me and I struggle to breathe. My vision goes black.

My Isabella.

I grab my heart and nearly fall. She was safe. Reading with Taryn. I left her only for a moment. How could this have happened? We had no word that it had begun. The dragons struck first. And they've already taken her.

It wasn't supposed to happen like this. This wasn't how I thought it would be. I'd only just started to love her as I always should have. I slam my fists against the wall. Over and over. My muscles scream and my knuckles bleed, but I don't care. I hardly even feel it.

They all stand around me, rising from the chairs, leaving the sound of the legs scraping across the floor echoing in my head. The vision of them, flying away with my Isabella flashes before my eyes. The bright green and pale blue scaled monsters. Their talons slicing through the bag. They fucking bagged them. Anger seers inside of me like I've never known as I turn and let my fist slam on the table. "They've taken them!"

"Who? They've taken who?" Carol stands next to me, closer than she should. She needs to back away. They all do. I'm caged in by the Authority.

"Isabella." I breathe her name and stumble into the chair. "They took her." The lump grows larger in my throat. The seers said my enemies would kill her. They'd come for us and take her. A hard slap across my face brings me back to reality. Carol's eyes flame with anger and a hint of revenge. Yes. We will have revenge.

"Who took Isabella?"

"The dragons. And Taryn. They took them both." My fists clench and my blood boils. My knuckles scream in agony. I could heal them easily, but I don't. I want to feel the pain. I won't let them; I won't let them kill her.

"Why would they take Bella?" Carol's worried gaze moves to the floor as the other members of the council question the situation.

"Why did the dragons come?" Rako asks.

"I've heard they were siding with the rebellion," Jared answers. Yes. We'd heard that a sorcerer was leading a rebellion of vampires and there'd been talk of the dragons.

But why would they actually wager war? They've been granted everything they ever asked for.

Why take my Isabella?

"Which rebellion?" Rako asks with a voice drenched in sarcasm. I stare at him with daggers. How dare he make light of this.

"We need to get her. I need to go." I turn to go to the door. I'll leave now. I can be there in less than a day and then I will get her. I must get her back.

"Don't be stupid, Alec." Carol's voice cuts through the air.

"I need to get her!" I scream so loudly my throat cries out in pain. "I failed her!"

"It's not your fault." Jared shakes his head and raises his hands. "I don't understand why they would take her. She's done nothing."

That fucking lump in my throat thickens as my heart lurches. "To get to me."

"You?" Rako asks with disbelief. The others stare back at me with shock. All but Carol. I'm not surprised she knew. She knows everything after all.

"We'll get her back Alec. We only need to find out why they took her." She speaks calmly and attempts to put her hand on my shoulder.

I brush her hand away; I don't want comfort. "They wanted to get to me. They wanted to start a war!" Rage lingers in my tone.

She doesn't flinch at my anger. She shakes her head. "No, that doesn't make sense, Alec." I start to respond, but she doesn't allow me to say a single word. "I need a week. I'll know why in one week."

"I can't wait that long." I push by her, but she slams the door shut in front of me. I scowl and turn my body to face her.

"Don't be a fool, Alec. What do you think you're going to do?" She walks closer to me, keeping her eyes on mine. "You think you'll walk through their city? Their devoted civilians will allow you to pass unharmed? Walk into their castle and steal your Isabella back without them knowing?" She tilts her head, mockingly. "Or did you think you'd fight them all and of course you'd win, because that's how true love and fairytales work?" A warning snarl rises through my chest as I unclench and clench my fists.

"I need to get her back." I fall to my knees with my head buried in my hands. "I failed her." I shake my head and look up to Carol. "But I will save her."

"We will save her. And in only a week's time, I'll know exactly how we'll get her back."

ABOUT WILLOW WINTERS

Thank you so much for reading my romances. I'm just a stay at home mom and avid reader turned author and I couldn't be happier.

I hope you love my books as much as I do!

More by Willow Winters
www.WillowWintersWrites.com/books